ALL CHANGE ON CRUMCAREY

CRUMCAREY ISLAND - BOOK 2

BETH RAIN

Copyright © 2023 by Beth Rain

All Change on Crumcarey (Crumcarey Island: Book 2)

First Publication: 26th May, 2023

All rights reserved.

No part of this book may be reproduced in any form or by any electronic or mechanical means, including information storage and retrieval systems. Except for use in any review, the reproduction or utilization of this work, in whole or in part, in any form by any electronic, mechanical or other means now known or hereafter invented, is forbidden without the written permission of the publisher.

Published by Beth Rain. The author may be contacted by email on bethrainauthor@gmail.com

❦ Created with Vellum

CHAPTER 1

PETER

'Scotland?!'

Peter Marshall practically spat the word out. Much to his annoyance, a giggle sounded at the other end of the line. His editor clearly thought this change of plan was highly amusing, but he was struggling to join in with the joke.

Gripping his mobile tightly, Peter did his best to reign in a sudden flash of anger. There was no point getting cross with Mel. The woman was bombproof, *and* she had the memory of an elephant. The last thing he needed was to give her any ammo for the future.

Besides, Peter knew he should be grateful... this was a steady job, after all – and that was about as rare as hen's teeth for writers... especially travel writers! Still, he was having a hard time disguising his shock. He didn't know why he was surprised though – it wasn't as if this was the first time she'd changed his assignment at the last minute. Yanking the rug out from under his feet seemed to be her favourite pastime!

'But you said-' he began.

'You're my best writer,' said Mel, cutting him off.

Peter could practically hear the shrug in her voice now. She didn't care where she was sending him – she just wanted him to get the job done.

Peter grunted at the backhanded compliment. He appreciated her belief in his work – he just wished it would lead to the bigger, glitzier jobs once in a while. Unfortunately, it seemed to have the opposite effect.

He'd worked with Mel for several years now, and he had to admit that as editors went, she was great. The problem was, she knew she could send him practically anywhere, and he wouldn't complain like the other writers did. He loved his job far too much to ruffle any feathers. The others were in it for the cash and any freebies they could get their hands on, but he did it because he truly loved his work.

'Come on Peter,' sighed Mel, 'we both know you're going to accept the job anyway, so there's no point pretending you're not.'

Peter grunted again. Damn, she really did know him far too well. Of *course* he was going to take the stupid job. It didn't stop him from behaving like a spoiled child who'd just had his ice-cream privileges revoked though!

Still – he couldn't pretend that the early morning email from Mel hadn't been a shock. He'd been preparing to leave for days. Finally, they were sending him somewhere he could expect white, coral sand, warm sunshine, and miles of empty beaches. He'd been promised a cabin by the sea and even a couple of palm trees to complete the picture.

So, when he'd gleefully downloaded his itinerary and travel documents, the words "Remote Scottish Island" had felt a bit like being slapped in the face with a slice of cold haggis.

A full minute of pure shock had followed before he'd typed the name of the island into his laptop. After all, he'd never even heard of Crumcarey, so he figured it was probably a good idea to have a quick check where she wanted to send him before complaining about its lack of cocktails and palm trees. "Remote" didn't really cover it. Mel was clearly intent on sending him to the middle of bloody nowhere again.

After a quick rant at his plastic pot plant, he'd grabbed his mobile, ready to demand – for once – that one of the other writers was going to have to take the cold, wet island in the middle of nowhere. She'd promised him the tropics, and she could bloody well give him the tropics.

'But... you made it sound like...' he spluttered at last, finally regaining his voice.

'I know, I know... I'm sorry,' said Mel, 'but I need you on this job!'

Peter let out a little huff.

'Look,' said Mel, clearly trying to placate him now,

'it's only for a few days – the locals are stumping up some of the cash to update their guidebook. I promise you, it'll pay off if you come through for me on this. I can't say too much right now, but there are some interesting things in the pipeline… and if you do this one for me, your name's going to be right at the top of the list.'

Peter pulled a face and started to pace around his sofa. Mel had said things like this to him a few too many times for him to take her word for it… but that didn't stop the swoop of excitement in his stomach.

It didn't change the fact that it always seemed to be him that ended up with the crappy jobs that no one else wanted, though. For once, he thought she'd come through for him and he was going to get to write about sun, sea and sand for a change.

'Whatever you've got lined up, it had better be bloody fantastic,' he muttered, still feeling mutinous. But he might as well give in. They both knew he'd go on this job, no matter how shitty it was.

'It will be,' said Mel, firmly. 'But for now, let's focus on this one, shall we?'

'Hit me with it!' sighed Peter, throwing himself back onto the dusty cushions and staring up at the ceiling. It was full of cobwebs. He really needed to start cleaning in between trips. 'What's the place called again?'

'Crumcarey,' said Mel, sounding relieved. 'It's off the north coast of Scotland. I've arranged for someone to show you around the island.'

'Oh *great!*' he muttered.

Sometimes local guides *were* great, but more often than not they were an absolute nightmare. It was quite a common occurrence for him to spend most of his trip trying to give them the slip. That way, at least he was able to get a proper feel for the place he was meant to be writing about, rather than having to deal with his guide's personal recommendations - which always seemed to involve their cousin's dodgy chippy or their best mate's seedy bar.

'You'll need them this time!' laughed Mel.

'I thought you said it's a small island?' said Peter.

'Oh, it is,' said Mel, 'but I've got a feeling you'll get a better feel for the place from the locals than if you go off on your own like you usually do. Anyway – I've had a look at their old guidebook. There doesn't seem to be much wrong with it, to be honest. The writing's a bit mediocre, so with a bit of polish and some of your magic… I can't see it's going to take much doing.'

Peter could see what she was trying to do – massage his ego a bit and she thought he'd trot off to Scotland like a good boy.

'Okay,' he said. 'Okay.' The second one came out as more of a sigh.

'Great!' said Mel, sounding relieved.

'Two things, though,' said Peter, before she could hang up.

'What?'

His editor's voice was wary now. Clearly, she'd

thought she was going to be able to slip away without him making any annoying demands. Well, tough luck!

'You've got me down as driving all that way?' he said. 'And then catching a ferry?'

'That's right.'

'Isn't there a plane I can catch instead?'

'Well...'

Peter knew damn well there was because he'd spotted it during his swift bit of grumpy googling.

'Yes,' Mel muttered. 'There *is* a plane but...'

'Don't tell me there isn't the budget,' said Peter. 'My car wouldn't get all that way, and a hire car would cost the company a fortune.'

'Fine!' sighed Mel. 'We'll fly you there. What's the second thing?'

'Send me a copy of that guidebook?' he said. 'At least that'll give me a chance to see what I'm meant to be improving on!'

'Of course,' said Mel. 'Right. Well... have fun!'

Peter opened his mouth to ask her a few more questions – but she was gone.

'Typical!' he muttered, tossing the mobile down onto the cushions where it bounced straight down the back.

Great. Another crappy job!

When he'd joined Worldly Press as one of their in-house travel writers, he'd really thought he'd hit the big time. At last, gone were the days of scratching around for freelance jobs that never quite paid enough to put food on the table. He would finally get the chance to make a name for himself by writing about some of the most glorious, tucked-away corners of the world.

Well... he *had* made a name for himself, hadn't he? And that was as the guy who could be sent practically anywhere at a moment's notice – because he simply couldn't say "no".

'Right!' he sighed, hauling himself to his feet.

There wasn't any point sitting there, griping about it, was there? He'd agreed to go – just like Mel had known he would – so he'd better go and pack. Or – in this case – *re-pack.*

Peter stomped through the flat towards his tiny bedroom, hoiked the carefully packed cabin case up onto his bed and opened the zip.

'What a joke!' he huffed, reaching in and picking up the first thing that came to hand. It was a short-sleeved, Hawaiian shirt. He tossed it aside, along with several pairs of shorts, his sunglasses and a pair of flip-flops.

Then, with much muttering, he replaced the jaunty, summery wardrobe with a pair of jeans and a couple of thick jumpers. Pausing for a moment, he cocked his head, wondering. It might be mid-June, but...

He bent down, and after rummaging through one of the large drawers that were built into the base of his bed, he dug out a bobble hat, fleecy snood and a thick pair of gloves. He'd been caught out by inhospitable weather before, and there was no way he was going to risk it again.

'Right. Ready as I'll ever be,' he huffed, flipping the lid of the case over and starting to tug at the zip. It didn't want to close – the jumpers were far more reluctant to play ball than the snazzy shirts had been. He'd almost managed to make the ends meet when he realised that he'd forgotten one key item.

Abandoning the recalcitrant case, he mooched into the bathroom and began rummaging around in the drawer where he kept all the random bits and pieces that barely ever saw the light of day.

He *knew* he had some in here somewhere. He'd bought it for his best mate's stag do when they'd all gone fishing.

'Bingo!' he said gloomily, yanking out a bottle of midge spray.

CHAPTER 2

ROWAN

'*You* want me to be a... *what?!*'

Rowan was doing her best not to let her voice rise to a pitch that only dogs and dolphins could hear – but it wasn't going too well.

'Don't be such a drama queen!' laughed Olive, polishing an already spotless pint glass as she peered placidly at Rowan from behind the bar of the Tallyaff.

'But... but...'

Rowan stared at Olive – and her friend stared right back. She dropped her eyes to the smooth surface of the bar and started to jam a fingernail into the grain of the wood. Olive promptly flicked her with the tea towel to make her stop.

'Just say "yes" Row,' said Olive, 'we both know you're going to eventually anyway.'

Rowan shook her head, pouting like a six-year-old. The problem was – it was very hard to say "no" to

Olive Martinelli. Not only had they been friends since Rowan really *had* been a pouty six-year-old, but Olive practically ran things here on Crumcarey. She was all-powerful… the queen bee of the island. Sure, she was about the most generous, kind and caring woman Rowan had ever met, barring her own beloved mother, but that didn't stop her from being just a teeny, tiny bit scary too.

Olive was on every single committee and steering group on Crumcarey. Hell, she even ran the little website they had going. Throw in the fact that the Tallyaff was the only decent place to go out for a meal and a glass of wine on the island, and it was best to go along with her plans!

'It's a job!' said Olive. 'I thought you said you could do with earning some money while you're here? And it'll be fun!'

Rowan pulled a face. Maybe it had been a bad idea to come back to Crumcarey after all. She'd thought it was the perfect place to find some peace and quiet – somewhere she could rest and re-group and lick her wounds while the office decided what they wanted to do with her.

With her big brother Connor away on holiday with Ivy, his new girlfriend, Rowan had practically bitten his hand off when he'd offered her his little cottage on The Dot. A cosy cottage on a tiny island reached by a causeway at low tide sounded idyllic… the perfect place to get her head sorted out.

'Come on, Row!' said Olive again, her voice taking on an uncharacteristic pleading tone. 'The old guidebook is a total joke. The guy who wrote it never even set foot on Crumcarey! He got everything wrong, and the pictures aren't even *of* the island!'

'You're joking?' said Rowan, her eyebrows shooting up.

'Nope,' sighed Olive. 'No one's really sure where he took them to be honest – but it definitely wasn't here. If I get one more tourist in here looking for our ancient forests, I'll-'

'Ancient forests?!' snorted Rowan, interrupting Olive just as she was about to get into her stride. She couldn't help laughing because there weren't any forests on Crumcarey. Hell... there weren't any trees! It was simply too windy. There were plenty of wide, sweeping fields and gorgeous old stone dikes, but definitely no ancient forests!

'So – what do you say?' said Olive. 'I need you to act as his tour guide. I need someone I can trust to keep an eye on him and what he's up to. We simply can't risk a mess like last time!'

'Oh... I don't know...' said Rowan.

She needed time alone to think, and if she had to babysit some random bloke and traipse him all over the island, she was going to have to be on her best behaviour. That was something she'd not been doing too well with lately!

'Can't you find someone else to do it?'

'I could,' said Olive with a frown. 'I mean, I have thought this through, you know. I did consider asking Mr Harris – but then the new guide would read more like a horror novel! It'd be all sharks and jellyfish'-

'And how to keep your hands soft and supple for milking the cows,' chortled Rowan.

'Exactly!' said Olive. 'Plus – you know McGregor doesn't really like strangers.'

Rowan nodded. McGregor was Mr Harris's dog. He had a reputation, though Rowan had only ever known him as the furball who appeared next to her feet every time she sat down in the Tallyaff for her Christmas meal. McGregor had eyes that could melt the most hardened heart – he could charm the pigs-in-blankets right off your plate.

'You're right,' said Rowan. 'That could be a bit of a problem… so maybe *not* Mr Harris.'

'I don't really understand why you're fighting this so hard, young lady!' said Olive. 'You're the best person for the job.'

'But I don't even live here!' said Rowan.

It was true – she was only here to make the most of her big brother's cottage. Now that he'd got so far with his renovations, it was like hiring the most gorgeous holiday cottage imaginable… as long as you didn't peep into the rooms he hadn't quite got around to doing up yet. But – it was free – and right now, that was the most important part of the whole arrangement.

'Don't give me that,' said Olive with a dramatic sigh.

'You were born here, brought up here, and if it wasn't for your weird desire for a bit of city life down south in Edinburgh, I'm betting you'd love nothing more than to grow old here too.'

'I'm only just in my thirties!' muttered Rowan.

'Clock's ticking!' said Olive.

'Crumcarey isn't going anywhere!' said Rowan through gritted teeth, deciding not to bite Olive's head off like she would have done if anyone else in the entire world had dared to utter those words anywhere near her. As far as she was concerned, the "clock" could go and take a running jump off Crumcarey's decidedly fake standing stones!

'No – you're right,' said Olive. '*Crumcarey's* not going anywhere. But unless we get a decent guidebook this time around to bring us some visitors who want to see what's really here rather than what's not, *we* might not be here for much longer.'

'It's not that bad, is it?' said Rowan.

'No – not quite yet – but it's definitely heading that way,' said Olive. 'A few visitors who aren't looking for our non-existent ancient forests would definitely be a nice change!'

'But... there's *got* to be someone better than me,' said Rowan.

'Okay – I didn't want to bring out the big guns, but you've forced my hand,' said Olive.

Rowan stared at her old friend, wondering what on earth she was about to come out with.

'You've been back for just two weeks ... and your tab is already overflowing with pastries and coffees. Plus, you're making a lovely dent in my collection of whiskeys too!'

Rowan opened her mouth to promise that she'd pay up soon, but Olive held up her hand for silence.

'Look – there's a small fee involved in this gig – I managed to get a grant. I mean, as the Chair of the Chamber of Commerce, it's my job-'

'Right...' said Rowan, not really wanting to hear about the inner workings of island politics right now.

'Do me this favour and make sure the writer sees the right bits of the island, and the fee's yours,' said Olive. 'I'll clear your entire tab, too.'

Rowan stayed very still, thinking about the offer. Considering the current state of her bank account and the rather precarious nature of her job back in Edinburgh, she didn't really have much choice in the matter, did she? Work was work.

'Throw in another pastry to go with the rest of my coffee, and I'll do it!' she said.

'That's my girl!' laughed Olive, lifting the lid on the glass dome and using a pair of tongs to place another flaky almond treat on her plate. 'I knew we'd get there eventually. Just remember – no ancient forests!'

'Fine, fine,' said Rowan, spraying a fine cloud of icing sugar and almonds as she took a huge bite.

'And make sure you show him the standing stones... and the ice cream van... and don't forget the puffins,' said Olive, ticking each item off on her fingers as she went.

Rowan rolled her eyes and nodded. Of *course* she'd show him her favourite Crumcarey visitors - they featured in some of her favourite childhood memories! Every year, she'd eagerly await word that they'd returned to their burrows on Craigie Head, and then she'd pester her parents until they'd agree to take her and Connor up to the cliffs to see them.

The memory brought a lump to Rowan's throat. She swallowed and blinked hard, willing the sudden heat behind her eyeballs to bugger off before Olive noticed. Luckily, Olive was still in full flow about the unmissable sights she needed to show their visitor when he arrived.

'… and don't forget Loch Crum and Loch Carey,' Olive finished at last.

'Are you sure you don't want to do this yourself?' said Rowan lightly, glad to hear her voice sounding normal, even if she felt like she was a hair's breadth away from bursting into tears.

'I'd love to – but there's no way I can fit it in. Traipsing around the island babysitting this townie…' she paused. 'I mean, you'll have *so* much fun. I just mean … with this place…'

Rowan shook her head and forced a smile onto her face. 'It's fine. I've said I'll do it – I won't back out now.'

'You can't anyway – you've nearly finished eating

the payment already!' said Olive. 'Oh, and don't forget the wine festival…'

'Why don't you write me a list,' said Rowan. She was joking of course, but Olive's eyes lit up at once.

'Good idea.'

Rowan just about managed to stop herself from face-palming. What on earth had she just let herself in for?

CHAPTER 3

PETER

The plane was little more than a flying Land Rover. There was no way this tiny, rattly tin can should be up in the air.

Peter was close enough to the pilot to ruffle his hair... not that he would, of course... that could end in disaster! Besides, it would mean releasing his death grip on the back of the pilot's seat in front of him, and right now that was not an option!

The only other passenger was sandwiched in next to him, so close that they were practically sitting on each other's laps. The large man wriggled around, reached into his grubby overalls pocket and drew out a small package wrapped in silver foil. He began to peel it open only to reveal a slightly crushed Scotch egg that instantly filled the cabin with the ripe smell of farts.

Peter's stomach rolled and his fingers tightened

reflexively as a gust of wind lifted the little plane by about a foot before dropping it again.

Why the hell had he insisted on flying to Crumcarey? He could be down there right now on a nice, big, comfortable ferry instead. Swallowing hard against an unfamiliar and rather embarrassing wave of nausea, he peered out of the window, eyeballing the tiny group of islands ahead of them.

Something was definitely… wrong.

Peter frowned. Mel had been as good as her word and had sent him the existing Crumcarey guidebook. In fact, it had arrived so fast that Peter suspected that she'd had it couriered the minute she'd put the phone down! Maybe she'd thought it would stop him from backing out of the whole thing.

If only he had!

The book wasn't actually that bad at all – just a little dated. It definitely needed a new layout, but luckily that side of things had nothing to do with him. All he had to do was check out the places mentioned, grab a couple of new photographs if things had changed beyond all recognition, and then do a very brief update on the words - which should be a doddle.

In fact, the arrival of the old guidebook had caused Peter to breathe a sigh of relief. He'd decided to treat this trip as a bit of a holiday – even if it wasn't quite the destination he'd been looking forward to.

Looking at the trio of islands below them now

though, he wasn't quite so sure. Perhaps it was the angle of the plane or the direction they were approaching from... but they didn't seem to match the map from the guidebook! He stared at the rugged scenery that was quickly getting closer as the pilot started to bring the old tin can lower in the sky.

'Erm... where are the forests?' he asked no one in particular.

'Not a tree to be had on Crumcarey!' laughed the man next to him as he scrunched the silver foil up into a tight ball.

'But... it says in here...' Peter finally released his hold on the back of the seat and tugged the old guidebook from his messenger bag.

'Oh – you don't want to believe a word that says!' laughed the man. 'Jock – he's read that stupid book!'

The pilot peered over his shoulder.

Peter instantly felt panic set in. Shouldn't he be focusing ahead... and... well... flying the plane?

'Good work of fiction, that!' said Jock with an eye roll.

'So – is that The Dot?' said Peter desperately, pointing at one of the smaller islands below them in an attempt to make the pilot face the front again. He *really* wanted him to focus on not crashing the plane!

Jock peered down. 'Nah! That's Little Crum!'

Peter opened the book and flipped through the pages until he found the map. It bore absolutely no resemblance to what he could see out of the window. He quickly turned the whole thing upside down, but it still didn't help. Nothing down there made any sense.

'Seriously!' said the other passenger, giving him a sharp nudge with his elbow. 'I'd toss that straight in the bin. The laddie who wrote it never even bothered to come to Crumcarey!'

'He what?!' said Peter.

No no no!

Suddenly, his nice easy job was turning into a nightmare before his eyes. If what they were saying was true, then it sounded like it was going to take a lot more work than he'd been expecting. Certainly more than Mel had let on. He wondered briefly if she knew…

Well, even if she did, there was no point throwing his toys out of the pram, was there? They were about to land. Besides, he had just over a week… that should be plenty of time to do *something* halfway decent. He'd just have to get on with it and make the best of the situation.

Then again… maybe these two were pulling his leg?

He glanced sideways at his fellow passenger, who was still watching him with an amused smile dancing on his face.

'You're having me on, aren't you?' said Peter, shooting him a conspiratorial smile.

'Sorry laddie,' said the man, shaking his head. 'Apparently, the writer thought he'd been to enough Scottish islands already. So he just made up a load of stuff because he wanted the fee. He knew no one would come up here to check. I mean, it's not like you get your passport stamped when you arrive, is it!'

He broke off to chuckle at his own joke, and Peter gave him a weak smile.

'Are you still talking about that guidebook thing?' asked Jock, turning to look at them again and shifting one of the earpieces of his headset. Peter had to stop himself from grabbing the pilot's head and forcibly turning him so that he was facing in the right direction to fly the plane.

'Yup,' said Peter, giving the book a nervous little wave. Why was he getting the feeling that the innocuous-looking slim volume in his hands was going to become an object of pure hate for him before too long?

'Don't worry, it's not just you,' said Jock, taking in the look on his face. 'That thing's been driving tourists mad for years.'

'Yeah!' laughed the other passenger. 'And the locals too!'

'Why's that?' said Peter.

'Because it's us that have to rescue the ones that come to the island and then get lost trying to follow that made-up map and all the ridiculous directions!' he said with a shrug.

'Surely the photos help a bit, even if the words don't?' said Peter, flicking through the glossy pages. He wasn't much of a photographer, but the photographs in there were lovely. He was hoping they'd still be able to use most of them. That was the plan, anyway.

'I think they're even worse than the text,' spluttered the pilot, finally turning back to look out of the front of the plane, though Peter got the distinct impression it was because he didn't want to have to look at the guidebook any longer than he had to.

'Why?' said Peter, with a definite sinking sensation in his stomach. This trip was going from bad to worse, and that was before he'd even stepped off the plane!

'Well… go to page sixty-four,' said his seatmate.

Peter flipped through the pages until he opened onto a gorgeous photo of a long, sandy stretch of beach. The sea was turquoise blue and the sand was white gold.

'There,' said the man, as if it proved his point without words.

'What?' said Peter, looking down at the photograph again and then back up to the disapproving frown next to him.

'Well… isn't it obvious?!' demanded the man.

Peter stared down again and then shrugged. Nope. It really wasn't obvious.

'What does the caption say?' said the man, now sounding like he was explaining something to a primary school kid.

"*Not Sandy* is a beautiful coral sand beach on the remote island of Crumcarey," said Peter, reading the words dutifully.

'And... with a name like that?' said the pilot, 'it's not likely to be a long stretch of white sand, is it?!'

'Oh – isn't it?' said Peter, considering the weird name properly for the first time. 'I thought it was just being ironic!'

'Erm... no!' came the pilot's voice. 'We're not really like that on Crumcarey.'

'We tell it like it is,' said the man next to him.

'So... where *is* this beach?' asked Peter. Because it really was glorious, so he'd definitely pay it a visit while he was here. Then he could update the words to go with the photograph and all would be well.

'About one hundred and thirty miles that way,' said the pilot. This time he didn't bother to turn around but thrust his hand out as far as the little cockpit would allow, pointing to the west.

'What... it's not even on Crumcarey?' said Peter.

'None of the photos are,' said the man next to him. 'Like I told you! And as for the forests, take a look below!'

Peter looked at the little islands that were looming larger below them. Rugged stone walls, fields, cows, sheep... but definitely no trees.

He let out a long sigh. This job was going to be a nightmare, wasn't it? And if the book was so drastically wrong about the forests and the beaches, what on earth was the little cottage he'd chosen as his base going to be like? Cold and roofless - he'd bet anything. It was probably that pile of rubble they'd just flown over – or the one over there with just a single wall still standing.

Or a tent.

If it *was* a tent, he was going straight back home. Mel would just have to get her backside up here and do the job herself!

CHAPTER 4

ROWAN

'Here,' said Olive, plonking a hefty cardboard box on the bar in front of her.

Rowan peered into the box and felt a decided twinge of jealousy. The care package Olive had put together to welcome this writer bloke to the island was a thing of dreams. Her dreams, at least. Peter Marshall didn't know how good he was going to get it. Olive had included most of her favourite things to welcome their guest.

The kitchen cupboards over on The Dot were running decidedly low on useful provisions. Rowan had slowly, but surely been eating her brother out of house and home. It was just as well she'd agreed to this job – however ungracefully. At least it would mean she could top up on a few luxuries rather than surviving on the bare minimum – namely Connor's stash of slightly soggy cornflakes!

Rowan reached into the box and snagged a little pack of shortbreads.

'No pilfering!' said Olive, giving the back of her hand a good-natured swat.

'He won't notice!' said Rowan with a cheeky wink, replacing the biscuits carefully.

'No – but I will,' said Olive. 'Anyway, I want him to feel welcome.'

'Olive!' laughed Rowan, 'you've included most of the contents of the shop in here – he'll love it!'

The shop at the Tallyaff served the entire island. It might be small, but it was perfectly formed and stocked with pretty much anything the islanders might need. There was everything from strong coffee to sticking plasters, fresh pastries to battery chargers.

'Well, it's important that he likes us!' said Olive. 'First impressions are everything, you know, and how he feels will show in his writing. That's why it's so important for you to be *nice to him!*'

'I promise… if he'll let me have a biscuit!' said Rowan with a grin.

Olive had been on (and on and on and on) about this ever since she'd roped her in for the job. So much so, that Rowan had started to dread his arrival - not because of having to drive the mythical Peter Marshall around the island to see the sights - but because after all the nagging, she was absolutely convinced that she was somehow going to put her foot in it and be the reason the new guidebook flopped.

It can't be worse than the one we've already got!

That was the thought that had kept her sane while she'd been waiting for the big day to arrive. Now that it was here, she was actually looking forward to meeting Peter.

'Right – you head off and get this delivered to Groatie Buckie Cottage!' said Olive. 'I need to clean!'

'Again?' said Rowan mildly. She could honestly say she'd never seen the Tallyaff look so sparklingly clean and organised – and that was saying something. Olive was a stickler! 'He's not even staying here!'

'No. He chose a cottage because he wanted to be right next to the sea,' said Olive.

'So what's with the cleaning obsession?' said Rowan.

'Shoo!' said Olive.

'Okay, okay,' laughed Rowan, scooping the heavy box of goodies into her arms and tilting it this way and that to stop any of the goodies from slipping off the top of the teetering pile. 'I'll leave you to get ready for the royal invasion!'

Rowan shot a final wink at Olive and swerved a good-natured pat aimed at her backside as she made her way out of the guesthouse and headed into the carpark.

Not for the first time, Rowan thanked her lucky stars that her big brother had lent her his car along with the house. At least it meant that she didn't have to borrow one of Olive's rentals to chauffer this Peter bloke around in. Somehow, she didn't think the whiff of cow or chicken poop would add quite the right kind of sparkle to his visit.

'Rowan. We need to talk.'

Rowan smiled at the old man leaning against her car. She briefly wondered how long he'd been waiting for her to appear. Mr Harris looked quite comfortable, and McGregor was busy irrigating her front tyre.

'Morning Mr Harris!' she said. 'What can I do for you?'

She'd bet almost anything she owned that it would have something to do with-

'Sharks!' said Mr Harris.

Rowan promptly bit her lips to stop a laugh from escaping.

'Sharks, Mr Harris?' she said at last when she'd just about got control of herself.

'Aye. Sharks,' he said with a decisive nod. McGregor finished his wee and turned to eyeball Rowan and the heavy box she had in her arms. She adjusted the weight slightly and stared straight back at the furry terror. She'd never seen the supposedly "vicious" side of the scruffy little dog, but it never hurt to keep an eye on him when he was watching you like that!

'You listening, girl?' said Mr Harris, taking an unsteady step towards her.

'I'm listening!' she said, with a smile.

'Good,' he said seriously. 'You make sure you tell that writer laddie about the sharks.'

Of *course* Mr Harris knew all about Peter arriving. This was Crumcarey after all! Rowan briefly considered pointing out that there weren't any dangerous sharks here on Crumcarey, but there really wasn't any point. She knew from long experience how many hours that particular argument could go on for, and this box was getting heavier by the second.

'I'll tell him,' said Rowan seriously. 'Now then – let me just pop this in the back!'

Mr Harris promptly moved to open the boot of Connor's car for her, and Rowan placed the box inside, thanking him with a sigh of relief.

'Nae bother!' said Mr Harris. 'Anyway, while the lad's here, feel free to ask me anything if you get stuck. Me and McGregor are ready to help!'

'Right. Brilliant. Thanks!' said Rowan, eyeballing McGregor again and making sure her hands were out of nipping range. She was half-tempted to point out to Mr Harris that she'd been born and brought up here on Crumcarey. Just because she'd chosen to move away didn't mean she'd forgotten it all.

Crumcarey was still her home – in her heart, at least. She adored it here… she just loved the bustle of Edinburgh, that was all. There was nothing better than a spot of people-watching. Crumcarey… well… it could just get a bit *too* quiet sometimes. The long days and even longer silences sometimes gave her a little bit too much time to think. And as for the memories... well, sometimes they were best buried underneath the bustle and noise of the city.

'Right,' she said. 'I'd better be-'

'There's something else you'll be wanting to share with the laddie too,' said Mr Harris, sticking his head into the boot and having a little rummage through the box of goodies.

'Oh yes?' said Rowan.

At this rate, she'd be lucky to be able to make a break for it in time to take this lot over to Peter's cottage before the man himself got there! She'd bet almost anything that Mr Harris was about to move on from sharks and ask her to give their VIP visitor warnings about jellyfish.

'If this is about the jellyfish...' she said.

'Not the jellyfish. But that's a good idea,' said Mr Harris, throwing her an approving look. I want you to tell him about my farm tours. I want him to add them to the new guide.'

Rowan raised her eyebrows. 'I had no idea you did tours!'

'I don't,' said Mr Harris. 'But if this laddie pops it in the new book, I might get a few visitors. And the cows will always put on a good show!'

Rowan had to bite her lips even harder this time. 'I'll... erm... I'll...' crap, her voice was breaking. The laughter she was trying to swallow down seemed determined to escape. She quickly cleared her throat.

'I'll mention it to him,' she finally managed to force out. Anything for a quiet life! 'Right – I'd better be off.'

Mr Harris nodded and patted the car before stepping out of the way. 'Don't forget where I am if you need a hand.'

'I won't!' said Rowan, quickly jumping into the car before he started back in on the sharks again. With a quick wave, she pulled out of the carpark.

Blimey – this job was getting weirder by the second. Now, not only was she going to have to show this Peter guy around the island, but she was also going to have to act as his bodyguard and protect him from Mr Harris. When that man got an idea in his head, it tended to stick. If he got his way, the old man would probably manage to wangle an entire section of the guidebook for tips on milking cows!

Rowan let out a huge yawn. She was knackered, and she hadn't really started yet! Winding the window down in the hope that a blast of chilly island air would help keep her awake, Rowan turned in the direction of Groatie Buckie cottage. At least its gorgeous old stone walls and cosy interior would guarantee a good first impression – even if everything went downhill from there!

CHAPTER 5

PETER

The touch-down had been... bumpy. If he was being completely honest, that was just the polite, British way of putting it. The flying Land Rover's near crash-landing seemed to have rearranged his entire skeleton, and Peter had to admit that if it was up to him, the flight would get a less than favourable review. There was no way he could put something like that in the book though, not in a million years. He'd have to come up with some kind of positive spin for it.

Jock the pilot had been endlessly apologetic, and Peter had done his best to wave away his words while silently hoping his spine would re-align when he got to the cottage and had a bit of a lie-down.

His inner grouching at the pilot's skill disappeared the minute Peter's feet met the solid tarmac of the runway. A gust of wind punched him in the side so hard that he had to grab hold of the handrail and hang on for dear life. Suddenly, rather than being mildly miffed at the bumpy landing, Peter was impressed that Jock had managed to set the plane down at all... let alone in the right country!

'Oof!'

The grunting gasp was forced from him as the wind redoubled its efforts, buffeting him against the metal rail.

'Alright there, lad?' asked his fellow passenger.

Peter nodded, doing his best to yank himself upright. He stared around. Right... so... this was small. As in – garden-shed sized small. So much for nipping into the airport for a coffee before calling a cab. It looked like he'd be walking to the cottage. At least the island was small – hopefully, he'd be able to get there on foot fairly easily.

'Can you tell me where Groatie Buckie Cottage is?' he asked, raising his voice over the wind.

'A fair step!' said the man. 'Maybe go to the Tallyaff and see if someone will give you a lift?'

Peter smiled his thanks. There was no way he'd be doing that. For one thing, he wasn't staying at the guesthouse, so it would be pretty awkward! For another thing, he quite fancied the walk. It might give his poor back a moment to sort itself out a bit while he got the chance to take a look around. That's if he could stand up long enough in this wind to put one foot in front of the other, of course.

'I'd give you a lift myself,' said the man, still

hovering near him, 'but my wife'll have the three grand kiddies in the car!'

'That's okay,' said Peter, his eyes starting to water as the wind whipped him in the face. He blinked hard. Maybe if he pretended there weren't tears running down his cheeks, the man would be good enough not to mention it. 'I fancy the walk.'

'Well – rather you than me, lad,' said the man with a smile.

Ten minutes later, Peter came to a standstill outside the Tallyaff. For a brief moment, he was tempted to head inside and beg for a hot drink and then a lift. Ten minutes out in this wind felt more like ten hours.

He eyeballed the heavy grey stone walls. The place had tiny windows, and on this ridiculously cold summer's day, with the clouds racing along behind it, Peter thought that the Tallyaff looked more like the setting for a serial-killer thriller than the cosy sanctuary it was meant to be.

He gave a little shudder, suddenly glad that he hadn't booked a room there. From what he'd read, the place had a sterling reputation but looking at it now, he couldn't help but wonder if that wasn't just another inaccuracy of the old guidebook.

Bending down, Peter unzipped the side pocket of his case and pulled out his fleece-lined snood. He yanked it gratefully over his head. Sure, it didn't offer much protection against this next-level wind, but it was something. Thank heavens he'd packed it!

Quickly rearranging his coat collar over the top of the snood in a bid to keep out as much of the biting breeze as possible, Peter grabbed the handle of his case. He was keen to set off again before someone spotted him. He wanted to get to the cottage and warm up. Or at least, that was the plan.

As everything so far had been the polar opposite of what he'd been expecting, Peter was dreading reaching Groatie Buckie Cottage. What if it was a total hole? He crossed his fingers inside his pocket that – at the very least - it would have a roof, heat and running water. He could put up with just the bare minimum. After all, he wasn't going to be here very long... he'd just have to rough it!

Letting out a long sigh, Peter did his best to tuck his chin inside the snood and ploughed on up the road. Honestly, why anyone would want to visit this place on purpose was beyond him. It was so barren. Considering it was almost midsummer, it felt more like he was back in the middle of winter. Grey sky, grey road, grey stone walls everywhere. The grass had grown into monstrous tussocks in the fields and everything felt like it was leaning towards the centre of the island... probably a result of the cutting wind sweeping up from the sea on a constant three-hundred-and-sixty-degree rotation.

Hmm. No wonder the original guidebook had been a complete work of fiction – how was anyone meant to say anything nice - anything alluring - about this place?

Grey.

Cold.

Barren.

Uninviting.

They weren't the most inspiring of words. He had his work cut out for him, that was for sure.

Now – where the hell was this cottage?

Peter was just cursing Mel and torturing himself with thoughts of sun, sea, sand and plenty of cocktails – when he rounded a bend on the sandy farm track he'd been following. He came to an abrupt halt - or at least he would have if the wind hadn't promptly given him a shove in the back and sent him stumbling a couple more steps forwards.

In front of him was a beautiful little whitewashed cottage. It was tucked away behind a low, stone-walled garden – but it looked right out over its own pebbly beach.

Okay – so he had to admit the place was decidedly cute – and it must have the most glorious views over the navy and turquoise waves.

'Bet it's grim inside!' he muttered, not wanting to get his hopes up.

Grim or not, Peter hurried around the corner, hauling his case over the ancient stones that led to the door. He couldn't wait to get inside.

When he'd booked the cottage, the owner had sent him a message to let him know that it would be left open for him – and although the keys would be on the kitchen table, there really wasn't any need to lock up behind himself when he went out and about. The whole idea had felt completely alien to Peter - sitting in his flat overlooking a busy main street… but now that he was here, it didn't seem quite so strange.

The only people he'd seen since arriving on Crumcarey were the ones who'd travelled with him on the plane. He got the distinct feeling that he could probably spend days here without ever glimpsing another living soul. Maybe even weeks… or months. He wasn't sure right now if that thought thrilled him or horrified him. Maybe it didn't matter… considering he was so cold that he couldn't feel his fingers.

He fumbled with the door handle, his stiff hands refusing to cooperate. After a frustrating fight, he finally managed to turn it and gave the door a hefty shove.

Success!

It swung open and a delicious wave of warmth rushed out to greet him, hitting him in the face and practically bringing tears of gratitude to his eyes in the process.

Peter hurried inside and then quickly turned to close the door, not wanting all the lovely warm air to escape. After the constant whistling of the wind rushing around his ears, the silence in the little cottage was almost deafening.

Peter felt himself slump slightly. He'd made it… and

from what he could see, it didn't look like his worst fears were going to be realised after all.

Dumping his stuff straight onto the kitchen table, Peter stared around, taking in the warm, carefully crafted wooden units, slate-topped counters and beautiful tile work. The merciful warmth was coming from an old, oil-fired range that took up most of the far wall. He made his way over to it, wanting to drop to his knees and wrap his arms around its gleaming hulk in gratitude. Instead, he turned his back on it and rested his behind against the rail, letting the heat soak into his coat and through his trousers. As he felt the backs of his calves and thighs start to toast nicely, he let out a long sigh of relief.

Well... he'd been wrong about the cottage. This place was lovely. It wasn't overdone - just cosy, comfortable and stylish. Even if the rest of the island was going to be a bit of a handful to write about, at least he had a nice base to do it from.

Then again, maybe he shouldn't speak too soon. He might find that he was in the one and only finished room. The rest of the place could be a bare, concrete shell for all he knew. Perhaps he should take his stuff upstairs and check it out!

Regretfully, Peter peeled himself away from the range and grabbed his case from the table. He pushed his way through a wooden door and out into a little corridor. It had warm, wooden boards on the floor – and he'd bet anything there was some kind of magical underfloor heating system at work out here. The cosy effect was helped no end by the fluffy sheepskin rug splayed out beneath his toes.

Making his way up the narrow stairs, being careful not to bash into any of the quirky photo frames that lined the wall, he found himself on a narrow landing. There was just a single door ahead of him. Was there really only one room up here?

He pushed his way inside and found himself in a lovely, light bedroom. Ah! He knew this place was too good to be true - there wasn't a bathroom!

That couldn't be right though, could it? Perhaps it was downstairs? Or... god forbid - was it out in the garden?

He dropped his bag onto the blue and white striped bedcover and peered around him.

Ah-ha!

There was another cleverly crafted wooden doorway hiding on the other side of the bed! Vaulting right over the springy mattress, Peter scrambled for the door, praying that it wasn't just going to be a cupboard.

It wasn't! The doorway led to a perfectly proportioned bathroom – complete with a huge, claw-foot bathtub.

'Well – that's definitely tempting!' chuckled Peter. He was still cold to the bone after being blown all the way there from the airport... but maybe he still shouldn't get his hopes up? Just because the cottage had surpassed his expectations so far – it didn't mean there would be any hot water, did it?

Holding his breath, almost daring the cottage to prove him wrong one more time, he held out his hand and turned on the hot tap.

'I knew it,' he sighed as the pipes spluttered and groaned before spitting out a stream of ice-cold water.

But... then... steam appeared, and the trickle turned into a torrent. A very hot torrent!

Scalding water was pounding into the bath, and Peter let out a loud cheer, which echoed around the white walls.

Right... so maybe this stay wasn't going to be quite so bad after all. He had the rest of the afternoon all to himself, so there was nothing stopping him, was there?

Peter quickly turned off the tap and then paused. He really should do something useful with his free time, shouldn't he?

But right at that moment, after a long, frustrating day of cramped travel followed by the walk of doom where he'd been frozen to the bone, the idea of a long, hot soak in this magnificent tub almost brought the tears back to his eyes again.

Making an executive decision, he grabbed the plug and popped it in the hole. Then he turned the hot tap on full blast, sending water tumbling into the bath.

The cottage was still unlocked just like it had been when he'd arrived. Maybe he should quickly nip down there and turn the key in the door? But frankly, he couldn't be bothered to go back downstairs again. After all, what was the point? There was no one around, and even the owners had suggested there was no need.

Without hesitating for another second, Peter kicked off his shoes, peeled off his coat, and then shrugged out of all his top layers in one swift move, leaving him standing there in just his jeans and the fleecy snood.

CHAPTER 6

ROWAN

Crawling down the sandy lane, Rowan let the car roll to a stop just before she hit the beach and pulled the handbrake on before killing the engine.

She glanced over at the little whitewashed form of Groatie Buckie Cottage and smiled. She loved this place - talk about sea views! Of course, it hadn't always been quite so cosy – it had needed an awful lot of work to turn it into the haven it was now. The owners, who lived half the year on the island and the other half abroad, had been happy to pay whatever was needed to bring Groatie Buckie Cottage back to its former glory.

In fact, it was Connor who'd done most of the work, so Rowan had been able to get sneak peeks of the work in progress whenever she'd come to visit. She'd never tell her brother for fear of giving him a big head – but he really did have a knack for taking an empty shell and turning it into something really special. That's why she'd jumped at his offer to stay in his cottage on The Dot. It might not be finished yet – but it was certainly a lot further forward than it had been at Christmas.

Rowan grinned to herself. That had been a decidedly no-frills stay! Back then, the cottage had boasted bare concrete floors and a host of power tools wearing paper Christmas hats. Now it felt a lot more like home. She had the distinct feeling that Ivy's arrival on Crumcarey had done a lot for Connor's new-found focus on getting the job finished.

Ivy had stayed at the Tallyaff with Olive to begin with, but the newcomer and Rowan's big brother had fallen head over heels for each other. It hadn't taken long before Ivy was staying on The Dot most nights. In the end, Olive had gently suggested that perhaps it might be a sensible idea if she took her suitcase with her and stopped racking up a tab at the Tallyaff for a room she barely ever used!

And so her confirmed bachelor of a brother had found himself living with the love of his life before he'd even realised what was happening. Rowan was thrilled for him – finding love on an island with less than one hundred inhabitants wasn't for the fainthearted!

Rowan gave herself a little shake. She needed to stop daydreaming. She'd take the box of goodies into the cottage and leave them on the kitchen table so that Peter would find them waiting for him when he arrived on the afternoon plane.

Holding on tightly so that the wind didn't wrestle the car door from her grip, Rowan pushed. It took every ounce of her strength to open it wide enough to sneak out without the entire thing being slammed against her by the gusts. Something you learned pretty quickly on Crumcarey was that you didn't stand a chance against the wind when it was having a tantrum, and you *always* held on tight to your car door!

Right. She'd quickly drop off the box and make a break for it. With their visitor arriving so late, she wouldn't have to start this ridiculous job Olive had roped her into until the morning.

Making her way quickly along the sea-view garden path, Rowan balanced the heavy box between her hip and the wall of the cottage so that she could open the door. Olive dealt with the changeovers for owners, so she'd already sent Rowan over the previous evening to make up the bed with fresh linen and turn the heating on – she'd been very clear about that - she wanted the place to be as welcoming as possible and toasty warm.

It's important he gets a good first impression, Rowan! This man has got our future livelihood in his hands.

Personally, Rowan thought Olive was overegging the whole thing a bit. Yes, she was sure it was important that this Peter bloke felt welcome, but frankly – he was going to love Crumcarey anyway – who wouldn't? Olive was worrying about nothing. Crumcarey was full of beauty whichever way you turned and whatever the weather.

Yes, there was a whole heap of downright fiction that he'd need to get rid of from the current guidebook – but there were plenty of gems to fill the new one with.

Fancy having a job like his! She was actually quite jealous of this guy – being paid to go to gorgeous parts of the country just so that he could write about them... she wouldn't mind a bit of that! It would certainly beat sitting in front of a computer all day fiddling around with numbers. Though, right now, she'd quite like to be allowed to get back to that, if she was honest!

'Stupid idiots,' she muttered under her breath. Perhaps she shouldn't start thinking about the office right now... it was guaranteed to put her in a bad mood!

Rowan kicked the cottage door open a little more forcefully than was strictly necessary and stomped into the kitchen. Bunging the box on the table, she turned back to the door and closed it more gently.

'Sorry,' she muttered. 'Not your fault.'

Wait... what was that?

Rowan stilled, tilting her head slightly. She was sure she'd just heard something. Wait... something was definitely up. She blinked slowly. The air around her seemed to be slightly foggy. And... oh hell... that sounded like the water tank! Had the system sprung a leak since last night? Maybe there was a fault with the range... could that cause a leak somewhere upstairs? That's where the sound was coming from.

Rowan hurried through to the hallway and up the stairs. She hadn't been imagining it – the landing was full of swirling steam.

'Crap!' she muttered. She paused and tilted her head again, listening hard to see if she could locate the source of the sound.

That's when she became aware of another noise. Strange and definitely out of place. A kind of high whining. It sounded like it was coming from the bedroom. Oh hell – had one of the joints in the plumbing sprung a leak? Soldering was definitely not one of her brother's strong points.

Hurrying forwards, Rowan let herself into the bedroom and then promptly pulled herself up short. It wasn't pipes whistling. It was singing – a painful bit of falsetto as someone did their best to murder an Ed Sheeran song in the bathroom.

Rowan's eyes dropped to the bed and grew wide. There sat an open case and a discarded copy of the old Crumcarey guidebook. Peter must have already arrived... and she'd just come very close to walking in on him in the bathroom.

Stifling a giggle as the invisible singer hit another painful high note, Rowan backed up, intent on escaping Groatie Buckie Cottage before the new arrival noticed her presence.

Crash!

'Balls!' she hissed.

In her haste to leave the room without interrupting

the less-than-dulcet tones coming from the bathroom, she'd managed to get her foot caught in the leg of the rickety bedside table and had sent the thing flying. On instinct, she ducked down, doing her best to shield herself behind the large, squashy bed.

The singing stopped abruptly – but the silence that followed didn't last long enough for Rowan's liking. Just as she was thinking she'd better skedaddle before she was caught on the hop, there was a great wave of splashing and sliding around from behind the closed bathroom door.

Before Rowan could even heave herself back to her feet, she found herself eye to… well… definitely *not* eye with their visitor.

Peter had appeared in a dripping rush, grasping a towel around his waist and brandishing a bar of soap as though it were some kind of weapon.

Rowan felt her lips twitch as a giggle rose out of nowhere. Her eyes trailed upwards from the towel-covered portion of Peter and drifted over his bare, glistening torso.

Okay – PHWOAR!

Rowan's eyes met Peter's, and she had to bite her lip to stop herself from laughing at the look of mingled surprise, fear and confusion on his face. She was just about to start explaining who she was and why she'd just wandered into his bedroom while he'd been mid-ablutions when the bar of soap made a bid for freedom.

Making an instinctive grab for the slippery little

sucker, Peter started to juggle with it, dropping his towel in the process and treating Rowan to an eyeful. She froze, staring. The bar of soap made a final break for freedom and slid right out of Peter's hands, hitting the floor with a thud before skittering under the bed.

Suddenly aware of his predicament, Peter followed Rowan's gaze south. With a gasp, he promptly did his best to cover his modesty with both hands. Unfortunately, his next move rather rendered the whole modesty thing moot.

Peter turned and dashed back into the bathroom, leaving both his towel and a wide-eyed, giggling Rowan behind him.

CHAPTER 7

PETER

Gah!

Peter slumped against the bathroom door, closed his eyes and watched an instant replay of the soap dashing out of his hand and disappearing under the bed. Then it did it again… and again as if his brain was intent on torturing him with some kind of weird memory loop.

GAH!

He wasn't exactly sure what he'd intended to do with it anyway! He couldn't have chosen a more useless weapon if he'd tried… but it was the first thing that had come to hand. Well, he guessed he could have lobbed it at his attacker and hoped to hit them in the eye… that would have been the best course of action. Instead, he'd just dropped it like the prize plonker he was.

The real question, of course, was why was he

obsessing about that bar of soap when he'd dropped something far, *far* more important?

Embarrassing, much?

Talk about trying to distract himself from the elephant in the room.

Gah! Unfortunate turn of phrase!

Peter opened his eyes and shook his head, but it did nothing to dislodge the pretty face with that pair of wide, staring eyes.

Staring at him.

Because… he'd been totally naked… and she'd been right at eye level with the aforementioned elephant in the room! And now, here he was, hiding in the bathroom without his towel. What was he going to do?

He could possibly dry himself with the bath mat, but that would be decidedly uncomfortable. Well, not *quite* as uncomfortable as what had just happened, but still pretty bad. Besides, he couldn't be completely certain that it was clean, could he? That would mean he'd be drying himself with something someone else's feet had wandered around on.

EWW!

Peter shook his head again. Was he seriously worrying about that right now when a beautiful if rather shell-shocked woman was standing right on the other side of this door?!

Should he say something? It wasn't like he could go out there and check if she was okay, was it? His clothes were on the bed, and his towel was out there too. He eyed the bath mat again and then screwed up his nose. Nope. He just couldn't.

A light knock on the door behind him made him whirl around as though he'd just been bitten on the behind.

'Excuse me?'

It was a female voice. It sounded rather strained to his ears, but he wasn't sure if that was because she was in shock, or because she was busy trying to hold back a laugh.

Peter covered his eyes briefly with both hands before quickly dropping them back down to their previous "shielding" position – just in case.

'Erm… yes?' he said, sounding *oh so casual* – considering he was standing there in his birthday suit. A birthday suit that was now decidedly covered in goosebumps - he was getting cold again.

'Would you like your towel back?' came the voice.

This was hell. He'd landed in hell, hadn't he?

'Yes please,' he said, his voice coming out small and resigned.

The next thing he knew, the bathroom door opened a crack. Before he had the chance to jump out of the way, a hand appeared around the corner gripping his towel between thumb and forefinger. He reached out and took it gratefully, before wrapping it firmly around his waist.

'Thanks,' he said to the half-open door.

'No problem,' said the voice. 'I'm really sorry to have bothered you.'

'I... erm... no problem,' said Peter, echoing her.

'I was just dropping off a few things,' she said.

'Oh. Thanks.' *Please go away so that I can get dressed.*

'No problem.'

'Right, so I'd better just...?' said Peter, hoping she'd take the hint.

'Sure... sure... erm welcome to Crumcarey! Enjoy your stay!'

Peter pressed his ear carefully against the door and was sure he could just about make out the sound of her footsteps padding back across the bedroom. He definitely caught the creak of the stairs and imagined her running lightly down them, no doubt eager to head straight back outside before the strange flasher she'd found in the cottage had the chance to strike again!

Peter closed his eyes and let out a long sigh.

Seriously - how embarrassing?

Basically about as bad as it could get – bar none.

There was the distant sound of an engine starting up and then he heard it pulling away from the cottage, presumably heading back up the little sandy lane towards the road.

Well... that was definitely a weird start to his stay here. All he could hope was that she hadn't managed to hear his terrible singing too! Peter frowned. Nope – he couldn't deal with that thought on top of everything else!

ALL CHANGE ON CRUMCAREY

Grabbing his newly re-acquired towel, Peter hurried to get dry and then dashed out into the bedroom. He pulled on his clothes, dressing in record time - just in case any more unexpected visitors appeared in the cottage.

One thing was for sure, he'd be making sure that both the cottage door *and* the bathroom door were firmly locked behind him before he dared to give the bath another visit!

Staring around the bedroom, Peter wondered what had made the crash that had brought him running in the first place. His eyes landed on the little bedside table nearest the door. It was standing at a slight diagonal as though it had been hastily set back on its feet. That must have been it!

He wondered what that woman had been doing up here in the first place. Poor thing – he hoped he hadn't scarred her for life! Thinking of those pretty eyes again wasn't going to help matters though, was it? It was too late to apologise now - she was long gone. Still, perhaps he'd get the chance to bump into her again while he was here. Then he could say sorry properly.

Peter ran his hands through his damp hair and gave a little shudder. He wasn't sure what would be worse – seeing her again and having to say sorry – or never seeing her again!

He let out a long sigh. There wasn't any point worrying about it now.

Anyway, hadn't she just said something about dropping off a box or something for him? Peter stared around the bedroom again, but he couldn't see anything. Maybe she'd left it downstairs. With one last glance around the bedroom, he jogged back downstairs and headed through to the kitchen. Sure enough, there was a huge cardboard box sitting in the middle of the table – and it looked like it was full to overflowing with all sorts of goodies.

Peter's stomach gave a loud grumble at the sight.

Plucking a little white envelope off the top of the food mountain, he slit it open and drew out a card boasting one very woolly sheep. For some reason, it was wearing a scarf. Raising his eyebrows, he opened it up, hoping against hope that it might give him some kind of clue as to who the dark-haired, wild-eyed visitor had been.

Nope. No such luck. He should have known – this haul was from Olive Martinelli, the woman who ran the Tallyaff guesthouse... along with the rest of the island from what Mel had told him in the notes she'd sent him. Olive was the one who'd pushed for the updated guidebook. She was also the person who'd been in charge of finding half the fee for the re-print.

Suddenly, Peter felt a pang of guilt for not staying with her at the Tallyaff when she was clearly going out of her way to welcome him to the island and make him as comfortable as possible!

Ah well – it couldn't be helped now. He'd nip into the dour, unwelcoming-looking place sometime tomorrow. He could go for a coffee – then if it was a total hole, he could thank her for the box and leave without seeming too rude. Anyone could put up with a bad coffee and a bit of cake in a dark, unwelcoming guesthouse, couldn't they?

Turning his attention back to the box, he started to rummage through its contents, spreading it out across the table. There seemed to be everything from homemade biscuits to tubs of hearty country soup, packs of coffee, and even a hot water bottle complete with a tartan cover. Blimey – Olive really was pulling out all the stops!

Right at the bottom was another copy of the original Crumcarey guidebook. Peter frowned at it. This blasted thing was quickly becoming the bane of his life. He picked it up and flipped open the front cover, only to come face to face with a bright pink post-it note covered with looping, even handwriting.

Don't believe a single thing between these covers. I know you won't let us down. Love Olive!

Peter smirked. Right... so, no pressure then!

Frankly, the more Peter heard about the original book and what a lazy hack job it was, the more he was tempted to demand that Mel and the others holding the purse strings at the publishers paid back every last penny of the fee. The islanders deserved a book that told the real story of their home – even if that was a cold grey windy wasteland surrounded by the sea.

He needed to get cracking first thing tomorrow and

start making a list of things to include in the new version. At least he would be able to wax lyrical about the warm welcome and the lovely accommodation if nothing else!

Suddenly feeling a heavy weight of responsibility at the prospect of the task now facing him, Peter slumped down into one of the kitchen chairs. It looked like his stay here on Crumcarey was going to have to be far, far busier than he'd been anticipating.

Reaching absently into the pile of food, Peter grabbed one of the many artisanal bars of chocolate – this one promising accents of black pepper and ginger. He tore open the wrapper, broke off a healthy chunk and shoved the entire thing in his mouth.

'Wow!' he murmured thickly, as the mad and delicious flavours melted on his tongue. Sitting forwards, he eyed the rest of the treats a little more carefully.

There – perfect!

He reached out and plucked one of three miniature bottles of Scotch from amongst its fellows. It might be a bit early in the day – but he reckoned he needed it for the shock.

'Bottoms up, old chap!' he sighed, cracking open the lid and taking a sip. It was peaty and tasted of wild moors and flickering fires… and it deserved far better than being necked straight from the bottle!

Hauling himself back to his feet, Peter raided the various kitchen cupboards until he finally found a decent glass. Pouring the amber liquid out of the bottle, he raised his glass in a silent toast and apology to the woman who'd delivered this box in the first place, then took another sip.

The warmth of the drink traced a smouldering line of fire from his tongue all the way down into his belly. Well... that was one way to warm up... and decidedly less embarrassing than his first attempt.

Picking up the useless guidebook, Peter settled in. He might as well know the full horror of what he was in for... though it might take his entire stash of Scotch before he reached the back page!

CHAPTER 8

ROWAN

'I thought you said Peter was on the *LATE* plane!' said Rowan, marching back into the Tallyaff and straight up to the bar.

'I did!' said Olive, obviously surprised to find the usually unrufflable Rowan looking well and truly *ruffled* and wide-eyed.

'Well… he was clearly on the early one,' said Rowan.

'Impossible!' said Olive, shaking her head firmly.

'Then why exactly did I just get an eyeful of his naked bum and… *other* things when I took that box over to Groatie Buckie Cottage for you?!' she demanded, trying to ignore the fact that her cheeks had just become ridiculously hot and were probably bright pink.

'Rowan!' squeaked Olive, wide-eyed herself now. 'I didn't hire you to *seduce* this man!'

'Oh hush!' said Rowan as Olive winked at her. 'You know damn well that's not what happened.'

'So what *did* happen?' demanded Olive, looking intrigued.

'Well – he must have arrived early and fancied a bath,' said Rowan.

'And you walked in on him?' gasped Olive.

'Not quite – but nearly,' said Rowan. 'I heard water upstairs and I thought there might be a problem with the plumbing – you know what those old ranges can be like!'

'Don't I just!' agreed Olive.

'Well exactly. I didn't want the poor man to arrive to water everywhere, so I went to investigate,' said Rowan. 'And he was in the bath.'

'How did you figure out it was him and not the pipes?' said Olive. 'That's if you really didn't walk in on him...'

'He was singing,' said Rowan.

Olive let out a giggle, and as much as Rowan was trying to keep a straight face, she couldn't help but join in.

'Was he good?'

'Decidedly not,' sighed Rowan. 'Anyway, I was trying to get out of there before he heard me, and I knocked that blasted rickety table over – the one by the bed.'

'Ah,' said Olive. 'That'd do it, then?'

'You could say that,' said Rowan, having to resist the

urge to fan her hot face with her hand. 'He ran out of the bathroom brandishing a bar of soap! He looked like he was ready to attack me with it.'

'What on earth did he think he was going to do with a bar of soap?' chuckled Olive.

'No idea!' said Rowan. 'Anyway – he lost control of it… and then the towel just…'

'Well – it's good the pair of you have met,' said Olive blandly.

'Met?!' squeaked Rowan. She wasn't sure that's quite how she would have put it. 'It was soooo embarrassing. How am I meant to work with the man now?'

'Ah now,' said Olive in a placating tone. 'I can't really see the problem, lass. He was just naked – that's all.'

'I *know* that!' said Rowan. 'I'm still trying to get the image out of my head!'

'That bad?' said Olive. She was smirking now.

Bad? Bad definitely wasn't the word Rowan would use for all that toned, muscular body with its smooth skin and…

'You're looking a little warm, dearie,' said Olive, promptly pouring her a glass of lemonade from the pump and setting it down on the bar in front of her.

'Thanks,' sighed Rowan, picking it up and taking a grateful sip. Maybe it would be best if she just didn't think about Peter without his clothes on.

'No problem – I'll add it to your tab,' grinned Olive. 'You know – the one I'm going to clear in return for you doing this job,' she added in a slightly sterner tone.

'Yeah yeah,' sighed Rowan.

'Calm down and untwist your knicker knackers,' said Olive. 'He's just here to do a job. He won't be here long and then you'll never have to see the man again. Anyway – how hard can it be to remain professional around each other for a few days?'

'Based on this morning – very hard.' Rowan sighed and gave herself a shake. 'Okay, you're right. I know – it was just a weird-'

'Cock up?' said Olive, her face completely innocent.

Rowan practically choked.

'Have a drink,' chuckled Olive, giving her a cheeky wink.

Rowan took a long sip of lemonade and let out a sigh. 'Okay – you do have a point. As much as I'd like to back away right now...'

'Don't you dare!' said Olive.

'I was just going to say... I wouldn't dare!' grinned Rowan. 'I've got my bar bill to think about.'

'And the reputation of your island home?' said Olive.

'Yeah. And that,' sighed Rowan.

'Excellent,' said Olive. 'Anyway – I'm glad you came back. I wanted to go through tomorrow's plan of action with you.'

'I thought it was just to pick this Peter guy up and

get on with showing him the sights?' said Rowan in surprise.

'Well – yes, it will be,' said Olive slowly. 'But first, I think it might be best to bring him here.'

'Into the lion's den?' laughed Rowan.

'I just want to make sure that this guidebook is the best it can be. After the last disaster, I'm not willing to leave anything up to chance,' said Olive.

'What, like an early arrival and a naked encounter,' quipped Rowan.

'You know I'm holding you responsible if he does a runner because of that, right?' said Olive.

'Not fair!' said Rowan, 'I was worried about the cottage flooding.'

'Well… as long as you were nice to him?' said Olive.

'Of course I was,' said Rowan defensively. 'I didn't just leg it straight away – I even handed him his towel back.'

'See – if you're brought up on the island, you know good manners,' said Olive.

'I'm not quite sure that's what she had in mind when old Mrs Kirkness was teaching us about manners in Sunday school,' chuckled Rowan.

'Dear old Margie – neither do I,' said Olive. 'Anyway – bring the lad here first. That way we can work out a proper schedule with him. We'll make a list of all the places you need to go and what to prioritise. It'll also mean we can keep an eye on what he does and doesn't see.'

'What – like Mr Harris's farm tours?!' said Rowan.

'Oh lord. I told him not to bother you with that,' said Olive.

'Don't worry, I'll do my best to keep Peter away from Mr Harris and his cows,' said Rowan.

'Excellent,' said Olive. 'And you know it's not because I don't trust you Row – I just want to make sure that he does Crumcarey justice!'

'Don't worry,' said Rowan, 'we will. So – I'll pick him up, bring him here to be brainwashed… and I guess we'd better tell him what we want to keep from the old guide?'

'Keep?' laughed Olive. 'That's easy – absolutely nothing. It's Peter's job to rectify every single bit of wrong information… and I think the best way to do that is to start from scratch.'

'Wow!' said Rowan. 'That's going to be a serious amount of work.'

Olive nodded. 'Yep yep. There's a lot to do, but he's here for more than a week, and I've been told he's the best writer the publisher has. His editor told me he's the one she likes to send when the job's a bit more tricky or unusual. Apparently, he's worked all over the world.'

'That explains a lot,' said Rowan, thinking of his tanned skin and gorgeous physique… and…

Stop it stop it!

'We need this guidebook to be a success,' said Olive, suddenly serious again. 'I know not everyone on

Crumcarey is happy with the idea of welcoming tourists, but the truth is – without them, we're going to end up with an empty island. We need the income, and we need the jobs. Without that, give it a generation and this place will be a ghost isle.'

'No pressure then!' said Rowan, her stomach suddenly squeezing with unexpected nerves.

'Oh – don't kid yourself,' said Olive lightly, 'there's plenty of pressure. That's why I chose you. I know you won't let us down!'

CHAPTER 9

PETER

Yawning and stretching, Peter wriggled down further in the bed, luxuriating in the gloriously warm sheets and fluffy duvet. Snuggling in again, he turned to stare at the flickers of light as they danced across the bedroom ceiling.

That had to have been the most amazing sleep he'd ever had. Not that he could remember any of it – he'd been out like a light. But waking up to the sound of the waves right outside his bedroom window was something he could definitely get used to, given half the chance!

Turning his face into the cosy pillow, he scrunched his eyes closed for a few more blissful moments, revelling in the warmth. If only he really *was* on holiday. He could luxuriate all he wanted to – but the reality was that just the other side of the plush, pastel tartan curtains was a grumpy grey island that probably posed the biggest puzzle of his career to date. Somehow, he had to figure out a way to transform its meagre charms into gems that would tempt the tourists.

Peter's eyes snapped open as a little wave of stress coursed through him, completely undoing the cosy calm vibe he'd been nurturing ever since the Scotch had hit just the right spot the previous day.

Sitting up, he tossed the duvet and blankets away from him and then winced as his now-cold hot water bottle tumbled off the foot of the bed and landed on the floorboards with the clatter-splat of rubber hitting wood.

Something about the sound brought back the awful moment when he'd dropped his towel and given that poor girl an eyeful.

Urgh – just what he needed – a shot of pure embarrassment to start the day off with a bang!

He really needed to keep his wits about him today. He was just going to have to do his best to forget all about the incident and cross his fingers that the pair of them didn't bump into each other again while he was here.

Heaving himself out of bed and sending up a little prayer of thanks as his feet hit the magically-warm floorboards, Peter pulled on his clothes. He would treat himself to a lazy breakfast with plenty of coffee – and then it would be time to walk over to the Tallyaff and visit Olive Martinelli. He might as well get it over and done with. Besides, after finishing reading the old guidebook the previous evening, he knew that he wouldn't be using a word of it. Any pointers from the woman who practically ran the place would definitely be a good idea at this point!

∼

Nearly an hour later, Peter reluctantly left the cosy haven of the cottage. He'd love nothing more than to hang out there for the whole day, slowly making his way through the box of goodies, and dozing on the huge, squishy sofa. As he pushed his way out through the front door, he instinctively hunched his shoulders, bracing his entire body for the impact of a howling gale… that didn't come.

Gingerly, he lifted his head and peered through half-open eyelids as though he was expecting to be hit in the face by the force of the weather at any moment.

The sky was… blue! The sun was warm and clear and bright – so much so that he brought his hand up to shade his eyes. The sea stretched away in front of him, calm and glistening as though it was wearing a multi-stranded diamond necklace.

'I've died and gone to heaven!' he murmured, staring around.

Where was the wind? Where were the unrelenting grey clouds and grumpy, uninviting sea? This morning, the water held the same turquoise hue and undeniable allure as some of the most exclusive seaside spots he'd ever been to. In fact, right now he couldn't think of anywhere else in the world that was quite as beautiful as this little stony cove with its azure water's edge.

Peter began to re-trace the walk he'd taken the previous day – and although he knew he was heading in the right direction, he barely recognised any of it. Yesterday, he'd focussed on the dull grey of the old stone walls and the uneven tarmac in front of him as he'd battled against the wind. This morning – with the sun shining overhead - he was struck by the wildflowers in the verges and the riot of unfamiliar birds that swirled and swooped over the fields, calling and squawking as they went.

As Peter wandered along in a dreamy kind of haze with his face tilted slightly upwards - as though he was determined to get as much photosynthesizing in as possible in case this moment of sunshine was a fluke – he became aware of a frenzy of activity going on around him. For an island that apparently didn't have that many residents, he was being greeted by an awful lot of people as he wandered along. What's more… they all seemed to be up to something!

There were hammers and scraps of wood in evidence, along with pots of paint and brushes… it was all a bit odd. After he'd passed what had to be the fifth or sixth front garden with someone busily daubing away with brightly coloured paint, Peter couldn't help but wonder if he'd managed to arrive during some kind of island-wide event. Yes – that was probably it.

He'd have to ask Olive about it when he reached the Tallyaff.

In fact – the guest house was just ahead of him already! How had that happened? Yesterday, the walk to Groatie Buckie Cottage had felt never-ending. This morning, he was actually quite sad that the walk was over so soon.

The Tallyaff itself looked far more inviting in the sunshine. What had looked like a dour stone barn the day before seemed to have transformed into a welcoming little haven. Of course, the effect might just have been because Peter really fancied another coffee! He quickly reminded himself not to expect too much. Still, a cup of instant coffee would be better than nothing.

With any luck, Olive would be able to give him a few pointers on some of Crumcarey's unmissable sights while he was there. He guessed he'd better ask her about this local guide he was being lumped with too.

Taking a deep breath, Peter plastered what he hoped was a polite smile on his face. One cup of bad coffee, a handful of pointers about the island, and he would be on his way.

He found himself inside a little porch, complete with a hat stand and boot rack. Surely they didn't expect him to take his shoes off! He peered around, looking for any kind of sign, but there was nothing. He *really* didn't want his socks on display right now... they might be clean, but there were definitely a couple of holes in the toes! It was hardly the impression he wanted to make. Peter prided himself on being professional – even if he wasn't particularly keen on the job in question.

Deciding to keep them on until he was told otherwise, Peter pushed the inner door open and hesitated, trying to take it all in. It felt a bit like he'd just opened a door onto an alternate universe. In front of him was a huge room, golden and twinkling. There was a bar at the far side, but this was much more than just a pub.

Morning light filtered in through the small, deep-set windows and bounced around the space – courtesy of some very cleverly placed mirrors. There was an abundance of lamps too, all of which were omitting a welcoming glow.

The Tallyaff was nothing like the grubby, greasy-spoon-style disaster he'd been imagining. There were pretty little tables set out around the vast space – their wooden tops polished to a golden shine. There was a huge fireplace to one side, and even with the sun shining outside, the fire was lit. The place felt warm and welcoming... though right now, it was also completely empty.

Off to the other side of the space was a kind of annexe that looked like it doubled as the island's shop. It was small... but from what he could see at this distance, it looked to be perfectly formed and ridiculously well-stocked. Excellent – maybe he could grab himself some bits and pieces to take with him so that he wouldn't have to return to the cottage for lunch!

'Are you coming in?'

The cheerful voice from over by the bar made Peter jump.

'Hi!' he said, spotting a woman watching him with a look of amusement on her face. 'Yes... sorry... I was just wondering if I need to take my shoes off first?'

'That depends!' said the woman with a smile. 'Are they currently covered in any manner of poo?'

'No. Definitely not!' laughed Peter in surprise.

'Well then – you can keep them on,' she said. 'And trust me – that's not always the answer I get! I'm Olive Martinelli by the way – and I'm guessing you must be Peter?'

'Yep. That's me,' Peter nodded, hastily stepping inside and closing the door behind him. He made his way over towards her, doing his best not to let the shock he was feeling show on his face. This place was as impressive as the cottage. He reached out and took the hand she was holding out to him, and promptly found himself on the receiving end of a very firm handshake. 'Thanks for the welcome package, by the way.'

'My pleasure,' said Olive. 'I hope you like the cottage?'

Peter nodded. Urgh – awkward! Was he going to have to start explaining why he hadn't wanted to stay here at the Tallyaff? Now that he was here, he had to grudgingly admit that if the rooms were even half as nice as the bar, he'd have been in seventh heaven here.

'I love Groatie Buckie Cottage!' said Olive. 'I manage it for the owners, you know. It's a gorgeous place to stay if you want to unwind right next to the sea.'

Peter smiled at her, suddenly grateful. It felt like she'd just read what was going through his head and wanted to let him off the hook.

'I did sleep like a log,' he admitted.

'That's good,' she said. 'Sometimes people are bothered by the wind when they first get here. It can take a bit of getting used to.'

Peter smiled at this. 'Only when I was trying to walk in it!'

'You should have popped in here,' said Olive. 'I'd have taken you over to the cottage, you know.'

'It was good for me,' said Peter. 'Good to stretch my legs and see a bit of the island straight away.'

'I bet you didn't see a single thing!' laughed Olive. 'I imagine you were too busy trying to stay on your feet!'

'Okay – you've got me,' said Peter, returning her smile warmly.

There was something about this woman that made it impossible not to instantly like her. She clearly knew the realities of her island home and seemed to be very straight-talking. Maybe she'd turn out to be a far more valuable ally than he'd given her credit for. After all, if he knew about the pitfalls that visitors to the island might encounter, he could include options in the guidebook to help them navigate the less-than-enjoyable bits.

If it's too windy to explore, head straight to the Tallyaff guesthouse for coffee and pastries, or even a three-course meal!

Of course, he'd have to sample the goods before making any such rash claims!

'Coffee?' asked Olive.

'Please!' said Peter, with the distinct feeling that Olive had just read his mind for the second time in as many minutes.

He watched as she turned to the giant, gleaming machine behind the bar. Something was telling him that this cup of coffee was going to rival any of the overpriced artisanal offerings he'd indulged in at home.

Two minutes later, the first sip of creamy, rich coffee was busily bringing tears to his eyes.

'Looks like you needed that!' said Olive with a smile.

'I may have rather enjoyed the Scotch you sent over!' said Peter.

'No wonder you slept through the wind, then!' laughed Olive. 'Definitely a good way to warm up, though!'

Peter nodded, taking another long sip of his coffee. Right... he'd better get down to it, hadn't he?

'So... Olive... my editor mentioned that she'd organised a local guide for me. Is that you?' said Peter, surprised to find that he was actually hoping that it was going to be her. Somehow, if he had the forthright Olive showing him around, he didn't think he'd mind it quite so much.

'Och, no!' said Olive with a tinkling laugh. 'As you can see, I've got my hands full...' she gestured around at the completely empty room. 'Or, I might have if some customers turn up. But I've got someone just perfect for you.'

'Oh,' said Peter, feeling the little bubble of hope disappear as fast as it had arrived. 'Great.'

'In fact, she was meant to pick you up from the cottage this morning to bring you over... so I'm quite surprised you're here on your own,' said Olive with a little frown.

Uh oh! This wasn't a good start. He hadn't realised that he was due to be chaperoned around this morning – but either way - whoever this woman was, she'd been late. It didn't bode well at all.

'Ah well,' said Olive. 'I'm sure she'll turn up in a moment. I'll make you another coffee when you've finished that one... and how about a pastry to go with it?'

'Thanks, that'd be lovely,' said Peter. 'You know – this place is a real hidden gem!'

'Some days, I wish it wasn't *quite* so hidden,' sighed Olive. 'Anyway – I'm sure you'll help fix that with the new guidebook!'

'I will do my best,' said Peter. 'You know, there's no

need for this person you've roped in to bother about me. Honestly, if you could just give me some pointers on where to start, that'll do... there's no need-'

'There's every need,' said Olive, cutting across him as she placed a flaky pastry on the bar, along with a linen napkin. 'Peter, can I be honest with you?'

'Erm – that's usually best!' said Peter in surprise.

'Well... frankly, Crumcarey is on its knees,' sighed Olive. 'The economy is stagnant, visitor numbers are down – and with that awful book confusing the ones we do get, things aren't getting any better.'

'I can imagine!' said Peter.

'Yeah,' said Olive. 'But it's not just that. Attendance at the recent wine festival was okay – but not brilliant. Of course, that's a lot to do with the conference centre and its... erm... less than appealing accommodation. That's a conversation for later, though.'

'Okay,' said Peter, grabbing his notebook from his bag and quickly making a note.

'Basically,' said Olive as she watched him re-cap his pen, 'we need visitors to survive – but they have to be the *right* visitors. People who fall in love with the island for what it is – and then keep coming back.'

'But surely that happens already?' said Peter.

'Not enough. Without the "ancient forests" they're promised, people start out disappointed – and then it's hard to change their attitudes. It's like... like they don't see the beauty right in front of them.'

Peter stared down at his coffee, feeling guilty. Wasn't that exactly what he'd almost done?

'We could do with attracting new people – both to live here and to visit,' said Olive. 'It's a really fine balance. We don't want to be swamped - because we simply can't cater for the masses. But, unless we start getting a steady stream of visitors and the income they bring to the island, there are going to be some very difficult decisions in Crumcarey's future.'

'Right,' said Peter, nodding even though he wasn't sure what to say. 'Blimey.'

'So yes,' said Olive, straightening up, squaring her shoulders and looking like she was ready to go into battle, 'there's every need for a local guide. I need you to fall in love with Crumcarey so that it comes across in your writing... and Rowan will make sure that happens.'

'Rowan?' said Peter.

'Yep. In fact, here she is now,' said Olive, turning to the door.

CHAPTER 10

ROWAN

Rowan felt as though her feet were glued to the carpet. A rush of fear crashed over her, and her heart started to race as the gist of what Olive had just said sank in.

Surely things couldn't be as bad as she was making out. Maybe her friend was just using these scare tactics to get Peter's attention and make sure he'd take his assignment seriously.

And yet... there were no customers in the Tallyaff this morning. In fact, as far as Rowan knew, there weren't any visitors other than herself and Peter on the entire island right now – and neither of them really counted, did they? She might not live on Crumcarey anymore, but she still thought of it as home... she couldn't bare the idea that the place she loved so much might be in trouble.

Rowan had always assumed that the island would

be there for her whenever she needed it – unchanged and reliable. She'd thought she could head out into the world knowing that Crumcarey would provide the perfect home that would have her back whenever she needed to feel its arms wrapped around her.

She hadn't meant to stand there eavesdropping for so long, but she'd been frozen to the spot by what she'd overheard. There was so much emotion behind Olive's words – and that was enough to convince Rowan that this wasn't some kind of show she was putting on for Peter's benefit.

Suddenly, a wave of guilt crashed over Rowan. She should have done more. Maybe it had been selfish of her to move away. Just look at Connor – he'd stayed on Crumcarey and as the captain of the ferry, he was a key part of making sure life on the island was possible. Not Rowan though – she'd fled to Edinburgh, citing the need for "city living". Only she knew that it was to escape the echoes of the past that came far too close for comfort whenever she was back here for too long.

Well – maybe this little job she'd agreed to would go some way to making that up to everyone. All she had to do was get past the fact that she'd already seen Peter without his clothes on, and they could make a start on things.

Not wanting to look like a complete weirdo by lingering half inside the doorway, Rowan moved further into the bar and made a show of shrugging out of her coat in an attempt to catch Olive's attention.

It worked.

'Here she is now!' said Olive, smiling over at her.

Rowan forced a grin. Suddenly, she wasn't quite so sure that she was ready to face the guy she'd seen starkers the day before. Now her heart was racing for a completely different reason.

Peter Marshall started to turn towards her, and Rowan felt reality slip into slow motion as the simple act of him swivelling on the barstool turned into some kind of momentous movie moment.

Racking her brain for an easy, light-hearted quip to lighten the moment, Rowan stared at him.

'You?' he said.

Oh. Well... that wasn't quite the positive response she'd been hoping for.

'Nice to see you with your clothes on!' she said, her voice sounding forced and strangled.

No no no! That wasn't meant to come out of her mouth! She watched as Peter turned an interesting shade of pink while Olive's eyes widened for a second in horror before she promptly dissolved into a fit of giggles.

Great. This morning was going *so well.* Quick... she needed to save it...

'Oh, and thanks for buggering off this morning and wasting my time,' she added in a harrumph.

Ah. No. So that might not have been the best way to fix anything.

'Well if *you* can't turn up in a timely fashion...' retorted Peter.

'Well, if *you* could just chill out and give a girl a break!' she shot back. 'I had a nightmare starting Connor's damn boat so that I could get over to Crumcarey in the first place!'

'Children!' snapped Olive, looking bemused. 'Quit it or I'll bang your heads together.'

Rowan promptly closed her mouth. You *didn't* mess with Olive Martinelli when she used that voice.

'Sorry Olive,' muttered Peter, sounding like an adorable toddler.

'Yeah, sorry Olive,' she mumbled.

'Not to me – to each other,' sighed Olive. 'Honestly!'

'Sorry,' said Peter.

Rowan just shrugged. She was not apologising to this rude son of a-

'Rowan!' snapped Olive.

'Sorry Peter,' she grumbled.

The man had the audacity to smile at her.

Cute. And Annoying. And too lovely for words without his clothes on. These next few days were going to be a complete nightmare!

'Right,' said Olive, giving them both a little nod. 'Now then – Peter – Rowan here, believe it or not, is the perfect person to guide you to the best spots on the island. She was born and bred here, and though she's only back for a visit, she'll make sure you see everything you need to – all the hidden gems.'

Rowan smiled gratefully at Olive, even though she wasn't sure what she'd just said was entirely true... but then again, maybe it was. She certainly knew the island like the back of her hand – and everyone who lived here too. Even though she'd been away for such a long time, not much had changed. All the places she'd fallen in love with as a child, and all the things that made this her home were still here. Well... *almost* all of them.

Peter raised an eyebrow at Rowan, and she felt her hackles rise.

'Don't worry,' she huffed, 'I won't get you lost if that's what you're thinking!'

'It's not what I was thinking at all, actually,' said Peter. 'I was just thinking it might be better if I had a local who actually lived here.'

Olive rolled her eyes at the pair of them again and shook her head.

'Nope,' she said with an air of someone not to be trifled with. 'In fact, that's exactly why Rowan is the *perfect* person to show you everything. As she said – there's no chance she'll get you lost, and she knows all the little nooks and crannies off the beaten path that visitors will love to discover – but because she doesn't live here, it's all still magical to her.'

Rowan raised her eyebrows in surprise. She hadn't thought about it like that before, but Olive did have a point. Being back here on Crumcarey was a treat – something to soothe her soul. As long as she didn't stay too long, she was usually able to keep the lingering sadness at bay. Maybe showing Peter around would give her the perfect excuse to get off her lazy behind a bit more and force her to revisit everything she loved about the island.

'Okay,' said Peter. 'That sounds great. As long as you're up for it?' he said, turning to Rowan.

Rowan glared at him for a moment. She was half-expecting to find a challenge on his face – but she was wrong. He was just being... polite. Like he wanted to check that she hadn't been roped into babysitting him against her will.

Well, he *might* have a bit of a point there if that's what he was thinking, but it was slowly dawning on Rowan that she really was the right person for this job. She could show him all the beauty Crumcarey had to offer – all the amazing things it was too easy to take for granted. She'd grab this chance to contribute to the future of her island home. Even if it only helped the tiniest bit, it would be worth it.

'Yes,' she said with a decided nod. 'I'm up for it,'

CHAPTER 11

PETER

*P*eter stared at Rowan. He was struggling to take his eyes off her – so much so that he must look something like a constipated guppy. She was just... gorgeous. Unnervingly so. Long, dark, windswept hair and eyes that sparkled like the sea had done that morning.

Urgh – listen to yourself!

So much for not bumping into her after yesterday's... incident! He frowned and tried to focus on not being a total knobhead for five minutes. *Why* he'd decided to go on the offensive and start picking a fight with the most beautiful woman he'd ever seen in real life was beyond him. But hey – at least it meant he wasn't completely frozen like a deer in the headlights!

Yesterday, it had been her eyes that had stayed with him... but he'd been in too much shock to really take her in. Today, however, he was weak at the knees. This could make things so bloody awkward. More awkward than the fact that she'd already seen him without any clothes on.

In reality, the awkwardness was the only thing he had against using Rowan as his guide. He needed to keep his mind on the job and having her around was going to guarantee the complete opposite.

Ah well – it looked like there was no point arguing with the formidable Olive Martinelli. Besides, he'd probably offended Rowan enough already to ensure that she wouldn't want to talk to him much as she marched him around Crumcarey.

'Okay, well – now that's sorted out,' said Olive, 'why don't the pair of you go on a bit of a preliminary drive around. Rowan – you drive so that Peter can get a proper feel for what's where.'

'Okay. I can do that,' said Rowan with a shrug.

Peter nodded. It would be good to get some kind of feel for the layout of the island. The flight overhead hadn't really left him any the wiser. He'd been too busy trying to match it to the map in the original guide-book… which was basically a random doodle worthy of a fantasy novel.

'And while you're doing that, I need to get an order in for some more stock for the shop!' said Olive.

'Had a busy spell?' said Peter curiously, struggling to imagine actual customers bustling around in here.

'Well, yes as it happens. It's been an unusual couple

of days in here, that's for sure,' said Olive with a bemused smile. 'There's something odd going on.'

'In what way?' said Rowan, looking curious.

'Well... I've had a bunch of paint here since the dawn of time,' said Olive. 'You know – the slightly dodgy colours, and little tins of gloss that no one really wants?'

Peter and Rowan both nodded.

'Well – they've all sold. It's been... frantic. That's the only word that really fits. And I mean, we're talking gloss, and emulsion, and... just anything and everything. I swear half the island must be on some kind of weird decorating spree!'

'Actually... now you come to mention it,' said Peter, 'I noticed something on my way here. I thought it was some kind of island tradition or something. Every single house I passed seemed to have someone painting outside.'

'What?' said Rowan. 'You mean decorating their houses?'

'No,' said Peter, shaking his head. 'They were all working on stuff I couldn't see... laid on the ground...'

'Well, we do have some odd traditions – but buying paint on the same day isn't one of them. I wonder what they're all up to!' laughed Olive. 'Even Mr Harris bought some violent pink silk emulsion.'

Peter's heart flipped as he watched Rowan break into a grin. Oh lord, that smile was going to cause him all kinds of problems, he could just feel it coming.

'What kind of traditions *do* you have?' he asked in a slightly strangled voice.

'Well... there's a law against Brussel Sprouts on Crumcarey,' said Rowan.

'There is?' he said in surprise.

Olive nodded. 'It's especially strict at Christmas.'

Peter raised his eyebrows, convinced the pair of them were in on a joke and he just wasn't getting it.

'Right... well... that's definitely an odd one,' he said.

'Well, whatever's going on with the paint – let's just hope it happens regularly. It's been the best few days I've had in the shop for months!' laughed Olive, starting to usher the pair of them towards the door, clearly intent on making sure they got on with the job in hand.

'Come on,' said Rowan, turning to him, 'I've got my car so that we can avoid... erm... I mean - just in case Olive needed the hire cars for visitors.'

'Oh – great,' said Peter, once again going slightly weak at the knees as she sent a smile in his direction. 'Thanks.'

Peter turned and gave Olive a bit of a pathetic wave before following Rowan out into the still-sunny carpark. They climbed into the little old car in silence, and the double *thunk* of the doors slamming seemed to echo in the silence between them.

'Sorry for-'

'Sorry I-'

They both spoke over each other and then ground to a halt.

'You go,' muttered Peter, embarrassed.

'I just wanted to say sorry for being a brat,' laughed Rowan. 'Anyway – I hope I've made it up to you a bit by saving you from Olive's rental cars.'

'Oh. That's okay,' he said, glancing at her with a little grin. 'And... why?'

'Well... one smells like chicken poo and the other like cow poo. Let's just say... they're not the most pleasant backdrop for touring the island!'

'Oh!' said Peter again.

Say something more interesting man!

'So... maybe not the best thing to include in the guidebook then?' he added with a hint of desperation.

Rowan laughed and shook her head, and Peter felt himself relax a bit. Maybe this wasn't going to be so bad after all... as long as he didn't look directly at her when she was smiling like that.

'What were you going to say?' she prompted.

'Well – I wanted to say sorry for... erm...' he paused and swallowed. This was going to sound ridiculous. 'I'm sorry for jumping out on you yesterday... and wielding that very dangerous bar of soap... and dropping my towel... and being naked... and...'

Rowan was giggling now, and Peter could feel the heat of embarrassment radiating from his cheeks no matter how hard he was trying to will it to bugger off.

'Don't worry about it,' said Rowan.

'I didn't know I'd be seeing you again. I thought you might just be delivering things for the shop and I had no idea you'd be my tour guide too!' he sighed. 'I should have chased after you to say sorry yesterday.'

'Well… that might have been worse, to be fair. You and that towel had issues to work out!' she chuckled.

'Yeah – you're right.'

'And as for not seeing people again on the island – that's basically impossible!'

'Right,' said Peter. 'So it's a close community then?'

'Everyone knows everyone,' said Rowan, nodding. 'As for jobs – there's loads to do and not many people around to do it all – so everyone tends to muck in. You just sort of have to get on with it here.'

She paused and Peter glanced at her. He thought he caught a flash of sadness pass over her face… or maybe he was just imagining it.

'Anyway,' she sighed, 'I'm sorry I didn't stop to introduce myself properly yesterday – that wasn't really fair on you. Maybe I should have waited downstairs, but I didn't think it was *quite the right time*.'

'You could say that!' said Peter, shooting a grateful smile at her.

'Cool. So – we're good?' said Rowan.

'We're good,' said Peter. 'Care to show me your island?'

'Let's do it,' said Rowan, slotting the key into the ignition and setting the car growling.

CHAPTER 12

ROWAN

'Right!' said Rowan.

She was determined to break the silence that had fallen between them. It wasn't exactly awkward... not really... but the problem with the word "naked" was that you simply couldn't include it in a polite apology without things getting instantly weird again.

It was time to make things as chilled and comfortable as possible. After all, they were going to be stuck with each other for several days – and she wasn't cut out for stilted conversation and walking on eggshells.

'I've got a plan,' she said.

'I'm glad one of us has!' said Peter, shooting her a grin.

Rowan shivered.

Naked!

There it was again... that word was trapped in the

car with them, flying around, bouncing off the doors and sunroof, and occasionally paffing her around the back of the head.

She cleared her throat and subtly wound her window down a little bit.

Focus, woman!

'Yep. So... I was thinking.' She paused and cleared her throat. 'I'll take you on a quick loop of the island. It won't take long, but it'll give you a feel for where everything is before we get stuck in properly.'

She paused and turned to him, but he didn't offer anything so she ploughed on.

'Anyway, that'll help you get the lay of the land a bit – then, we can go back to Olive's, scrounge another coffee and a spot of lunch – and make a plan of action in terms of what needs to go in the book?'

Peter stared at her.

'Or... you know... whatever you want to do?' she said. 'Sorry – Connor says I get bossy when I'm on a roll!'

'Connor?' said Peter, sounding slightly dazed.

'My big brother,' said Rowan, rolling her eyes. She loved Connor dearly, but the pair of them bickered like primary school kids whenever they were within pinching distance of each other. 'I'm staying in his cottage while I'm here. He and his new girlfriend are off being sickeningly cute on another continent at the moment!'

'Don't you like her?' asked Peter.

'Ivy? I adore her! In my humble opinion, she's the best thing ever to happen to my idiot brother,' she said. 'Actually – Ivy's like a poster girl for Crumcarey magic. She arrived at Christmas, got stranded… and basically moved her entire life here without ever setting foot back on the mainland.'

'You're not serious?' said Peter.

'Deadly serious,' said Rowan. 'The girl's nuts. She got her friends to pack all her stuff and ship it up to her. She'd left her car over at the airport on the mainland but Jock – the pilot – got stuck over there when the plane needed some work, so he drove Ivy's car up to the coast and brought it back over on the ferry!'

'Blimey,' said Peter. 'I'd better get my guard up then!'

'How so?' said Rowan.

'I don't want any of that magic island fairy dust making me stay put. I like exploring too much for that!' he said, shooting her a smile that made her squirm in her seat.

'Is that why you do this as a job?' said Rowan.

'Yep!' said Peter. 'I get to travel all over.'

'But you don't get to choose where you go?' said Rowan.

'Well… no,' said Peter.

'So you don't really want to be here on Crumcarey?' said Rowan.

She wasn't sure why she needed to know this… but she definitely got the sense that Peter wasn't quite up for this assignment. It was something in the way Olive had been so worried about making sure he got the right first impression – she definitely seemed to think that he might be a flight risk.

'It's not that,' said Peter, ruffling his hair and looking awkward. 'Honestly!' he added when she frowned at him. 'It's just that my editor had told me I was off to the tropics. I was all packed and ready to go, and then she swapped me out for another writer at the last minute. So here I am.'

'Not quite the tropics,' said Rowan, nodding her head.

'Still… lovely though?' said Peter, not sounding quite as convinced as she would like.

Crumcarey *was* lovely, but she needed to make sure he saw that too, otherwise that tinge of negativity was bound to find its way into his writing, wasn't it?! And from what she'd overheard that morning in the Tallyaff, they couldn't afford for that to happen.

'It is lovely here,' she said. 'It's definitely *not* the tropics, but this place really does have a magic all of its own… it's why I always come back when I need to get my head straight.'

'Is that why you're here now?' said Peter. 'Getting your head straight?'

Damnit! Why had she just said that out loud?! It was the last thing she wanted to talk about right now. She needed to keep this light, airy and positive, and her reasons for camping out in Connor's house were anything but.

'Just a little holiday,' she said, doing her best to sound breezy.

'Ooh look!' said Peter, pointing ahead and then quickly rummaging in his bag for his notebook. 'Now there's something that looks like it belongs in the guidebook!'

Rowan sent up a quick prayer of thanks that he'd been distracted before she'd had to explain exactly why she was here on the island… though she had no idea what he was getting all excited about. It was just Mr Harris's farm!

'I had no idea the island would have a petting zoo!' said Peter. 'And farm tours too?!'

'Honestly… neither did I,' giggled Rowan as Peter quickly scribbled a few sentences in his notepad.

Mr Harris had put up a new sign since she'd driven past on her way to the Tallyaff that morning. Rowan let out a surprised yelp of laughter.

'What's so funny?' said Peter, looking confused as she showed no sign of slowing down.

'Because that's Mr Harris's place,' she said shaking her head.

'And?' said Peter.

'And I think we might be getting to the bottom of where all Olive's paint's been going!' said Rowan.

The sign was about six feet high and painted on what looked to be a bunch of old pallets piled against each other. They'd been daubed with a rainbow of metallic purple and violent pink paint. It was basically a huge price list.

'Blimey!' she said. 'That would be daylight robbery even if he did have "bunnies and llamas" ready for a "cuddle experience"!'

'You mean... it's not a petting zoo?' said Peter.

'Not last time I checked!' laughed Rowan. 'He's got some very lovely and rather spoiled cows... but that's about it. Though I'm sure he'd gladly take twenty-five quid in return for letting you wander around his fields while he regales you with advice on how to keep your hands soft for the best tasting milk!'

'Erm... maybe we'll give it a miss then?' said Peter, promptly crossing out the notes he'd just made.

'Good call,' said Rowan, speeding up a little bit. The sooner she showed Peter some of the *actual* sights, the better!

~

Just over half an hour later, things were getting more than a little bit embarrassing. As per her plan, Rowan had pointed out the beaches - Big Sandy, Small Sandy and Not Sandy. Then she'd swung past The Dot. The tide was still in, and Connor's little boat sat moored where she'd left it, ready to take her back over to the cottage should she want to return before the causeway became passable again.

Peter had been quite excited about the standing stones. Rowan loved them herself, so she felt like a complete party pooper when she'd had to tell him they'd only been put up when she was a kid as an April Fool's joke.

It wasn't the fake standing stones that she was worried about right now though, nor the less-than-stellar comments she'd had to share about the grotty accommodation at the conference centre. Nope – it was the signs. It wasn't just Mr Harris that had decided to reinvent himself. They were everywhere!

'Another café?' asked Peter, nodding at a red and green glossed monstrosity.

'Nope,' sighed Rowan, shifting in her seat.

'Right,' said Peter with a sigh.

He looked more than a little bit bewildered and Rowan couldn't blame him. It was probably the tenth sign for a café they'd passed in as many minutes. This one had been painted on an old bit of wallpaper and it was hanging from Mrs Costie's garden gate.

Rowan knew full well that the best Peter would get out of Mrs Costie was a quick cup of instant and maybe a soggy custard cream if he was lucky. What he definitely *would* get was an enforced trawl through Mrs Costie's family photo albums while she kept him hostage on her large, squashy floral sofa. To add insult to injury, the sofa was always covered in more cats than was strictly necessary for such a tiny cottage.

Rowan had actually been getting quite excited to

show Peter some of Crumcarey's *real* hidden gems – but the poor guy looked totally deflated by this point.

'You look confused,' she said.

'A bit!' said Peter, shooting her a small smile.

Rowan couldn't blame him. By this point, she thought she had a fairly good idea as to what was going on, but she'd save that conversation for when they were safely back in the Tallyaff with a coffee and a sweet treat in front of them!

'Ooh - how about this one, though?' said Peter, perking up. 'We're definitely going to stop here, right? I mean, the island's museum must be pretty important!'

Rowan glanced across to see what he was looking at. It was Mr McClusky's house – complete with yet another newly painted sign.

Crumcarey Museum

Rowan snorted.

'Should I at least write down the location for my notes?' he asked.

Rowan shook her head and carried on driving.

'There isn't really a museum there,' she said. 'He's got a barn full of old junk out the back – and trust me, none of it is particularly old or noteworthy. He just hasn't forked out and hired a skip for a long time!'

'Oh,' said Peter, deflating again.

Rowan sighed. They were nearly back to the beginning of their island loop. That coffee and a bit of cake couldn't come soon enough as far as Rowan was concerned. This preliminary trip had been a total disaster.

'Look – let's head back to the Tallyaff. We need a new plan,' said Rowan.

Peter just nodded.

'And that's really not a cinema,' sighed Rowan, rolling her eyes as Mrs Rendall's cottage came into view.

Crumcarey's Famous Vintage Cinema.

'And it's definitely *not* famous!'

'I guessed,' said Peter.

'Yeah. She's just got a really big old TV – one of those monsters that came in its own cabinet and needs a crane to move it around.'

'Right,' said Peter. 'At least she's done a nice job with the sign, though,' he added.

Rowan nodded. There was bunting painted all the way along the top of this one… but it didn't change the fact that it was basically just advertising a TV in a living room.

'Hate to tell you this,' said Rowan, 'but the TV doesn't even work anymore… and it was black and white when it did.'

Peter let out a snort of laughter. Clearly giving the whole thing up as a bad job, he slipped his notepad back into his bag looking totally defeated.

CHAPTER 13

PETER

*P*eter followed Rowan across the empty carpark towards the Tallyaff. He'd been hoping that their drive around the island would give him plenty of starting points for the new guidebook – but all he'd managed to get from the experience were several pages of scribbled-out notes and a pounding headache.

He couldn't deny the fact that there was a hint of panic starting to creep in. Even though he hadn't been keen on this trip to begin with, now that he was here, he was desperate to make a good job of it... especially after what Olive had told him earlier.

The problem was, with all these false businesses and fake standing stones, his head was spinning. The entire island was like a jumbled mess in his head and he was starting to doubt his ability to pull together something that was both truthful and enticing. Perhaps

Crumcarey simply wasn't a place that was made for tourists after all.

With a sinking sensation, he followed Rowan back into the bar. It was the last place he wanted to be right now – not that he'd ever admit it. He was craving the peace and solitude of his little seaside cottage. A coffee... and then a lie down with the heavy curtains drawn would be right up his street. But no – he was a professional, wasn't he? He needed to get to work and figure this out After all, Rowan loved this place... so there must be something to write about.

'You two are back early!' said Olive in surprise. She was busy stocking the bakery shelves and straightened up to stare at them with her tongs in hand.

'We've figured out what all your paint's been used for!' said Rowan, with a rueful smile.

'Oh?' said Olive.

'Yeah,' sighed Peter. 'The island now has about ten other cafes, a petting zoo, a museum and a cinema... and Rowan wouldn't let me visit any of them!'

'Wait,' said Olive, looking about as confused as Peter felt. 'What's that now?'

'Can we get a couple of pastries?' said Rowan. 'And maybe a coffee? I think Peter needs the sugar after all that!'

'Sure!' said Olive. 'And... maybe explain what you're both on about while I'm at it?' said Olive, carrying the basket of pastries back over to the bar.

'Well,' said Rowan, hot on Olive's heels, 'I'd say everyone might have cottoned onto Peter's visit.'

Peter raised his eyebrows and slumped down onto one of the bar stools. 'You're saying that was all for my benefit?'

'I reckon so!' said Rowan with a chuckle.

'What was?!' demanded Olive.

Rowan quickly filled her in while Peter wrapped his hands around the mug of coffee Olive placed in front of him. He was only just about managing to resist the temptation to rest his forehead on the bar and either take a nap or have a little cry.

It didn't take long before Olive was laughing – and she let out a particularly loud hoot when Rowan described Mr Harris's brand new petting zoo.

'You've got to hand it to them – you can't fault them for trying!' said Olive.

'That's true,' said Rowan, her eyes shining. 'To be honest I'm a bit gutted – I'd quite like to have spent the morning cuddling some lamas.'

Peter let out a splutter of laughter. He couldn't help it.

'Maybe Mr Harris can be persuaded to actually give the whole farm tour thing a go for real!' he said.

'Oh don't!' said Olive, wiping her eyes. 'I can just imagine it... and with that monkey of a McGregor going for everyone who dared visit.'

'Mr Harris's dog,' said Rowan, taking pity on him and explaining before he even had to ask.

'Anyway,' said Olive. 'I'm guessing it was probably Mr Harris who spread the word about what you were here to do, Peter.'

'Problem is,' said Rowan, 'it's all a bit… confusing.'

Peter nodded. Confusing was definitely the word for it. Not only did he have no clue what the real attractions were, he also still didn't have the foggiest about the lay of the land. Their little road trip had only served to completely befuddle him.

Plus, being in the confined space with Rowan for so long, with her light, citrus perfume making his senses tingle hadn't helped matters.

'What you need is a map,' said Olive. 'And not that made-up one in the old book.'

'I guess it would be a good start,' said Peter.

He was just trying to be polite by this point. There was no way a map was going to be much help… not if there wasn't actually anything much for visitors to see here!

'Right,' said Olive. 'Two secs!'

Peter watched her disappear out through the back door and turned to Rowan.

'Honestly – I'm not so sure a map will help,' he muttered.

'We'll make it work, don't worry,' she said.

Peter nodded. She sounded determined, and something told Peter that he'd be better off just going along with whatever the pair of them cooked up for now. He could always figure out a way to explore the island on his own later. Right now, he needed all the help he could get if he wasn't going to end up drinking tea with a bunch of cats sitting on him!

'Right – here we go!' said Olive, reappearing and flourishing a massive flip-pad of paper in front of her.

She made her way over to one of the dining tables, cleared away the place settings and condiment basket from the middle and gave the wood a hasty wipe-over with the sleeve of her cardigan. Then she dropped the paper onto the surface.

With a quiet sigh, Peter hopped down from his chair and wandered over to take a look at the map.

'Oh!' he said in surprise. It was just a large sheet of blank paper.

'Rowan,' said Olive, bustling back over to the bar, 'care to do the honours?'

Peter watched in confusion as she bent down and then reappeared with a large, canary-yellow pencil case.

'Oh... erm... no,' said Rowan. 'I don't think-'

'Well, Peter can't do it, can he?' said Olive. 'And you know anything I try to draw always looks like a demented duck.'

Without waiting for Rowan to respond, Olive tossed the pencil case with a throw worthy of a rugby player. Acting on instinct, Rowan snatched it deftly from mid-air. She unzipped it slowly and drew out a thick, dark pencil, looking like she thought it might bite her.

'Watch this,' Olive muttered in Peter's ear as she came to stand next to him. 'You want to see the wonders of Crumcarey? One of them is standing right in front of you.'

Peter raised his eyebrows in a silent question, but Olive just nodded, urging him to turn his attention back to Rowan.

'Right...' muttered Rowan, tapping the chunky pencil against her chin and staring intently at the blank page in front of her. 'What do we need... the three islands first, I guess.'

Peter watched as Rowan's hand started to fly across the surface of the paper, her strokes sure and fluid. He'd never seen anyone draw like this before – it looked so easy and unflustered.

It wasn't long before there were three little islands complete with beautifully depicted details, and he began to recognise some of the landmarks they'd passed on their disastrous tour that morning.

'Don't forget Stella's van!' said Olive, craning her neck.

'Of course!' said Rowan, not taking her eyes off the map in front of her as she drew a beautiful vintage ice cream van to one side and added a sleek arrow pointing towards Big Sandy.

Next, she drew her brother's house on The Dot, the tiny island separated from Crumcarey by a tidal causeway.

'I'll need to show you the best spot for Groatie

Buckie hunting too!' murmured Rowan, clearly engrossed as her pencil drew several sure curves.

'But I know where my cottage is!' said Peter, half-mesmerised by what was going on in front of him.

'Your cottage is named after Groatie Buckie shells!' said Olive. 'Lovely little cowrie shells... they're lucky, you know, but little blighters to find until you get your eye in!'

'And you need to know the best spots!' said Rowan.

The curves had morphed into an unmistakable cowrie shell, with its tell-tale opening and fine ridges. Rowan swifty added an arrow that led to a rocky outcrop to the west side of the island.

'Then there are the standing stones, of course,' she said, adding the stone ring at the centre of the island.

'I thought you said those were fake!' said Peter.

'Well... they are,' said Olive, 'but folks seem to really like them anyway... and all good traditions have to start somewhere, don't they?'

'It's pretty at sunset!' said Rowan. 'I quite like to take a blanket up there and watch the stars come out. Connor thinks I'm an idiot, but it's really magical. I reckon folks would love to see them!'

Peter nodded. He suddenly wished he had his notebook in his hands... mostly so that he could use it to hide his face. He was pretty sure he was blushing right now because all he really wanted to do was ask if he could join Rowan under her blanket!

'It's ridiculous that none of this was in the first

guide!' he muttered. His panic was starting to subside. There was already quite a lot here he could work with!

'Exactly,' said Olive, an angry bite to her voice. 'I mean – not all tourists are made equal, are they? I know we won't be everyone's cup of tea, but there's plenty of magic to be found here for the right people.'

Peter nodded as he watched Rowan drawing a perfect pair of puffins above a rocky sea stack. The map had taken shape right in front of his eyes.

'Well,' he said, 'clearly that other writer was an idiot.'

Sure, Peter had to admit that he hadn't been that keen to come to Crumcarey himself – but he hated to think how close he'd come to missing this. There really *was* something magical to see here on this little island… and that was Rowan!

CHAPTER 14

ROWAN

Rowan flung the pencil away from her and shoved her chair back from the table. There. She was done. That would just have to do!

She stood up and retreated a couple of paces, breathing hard as though she'd just run a marathon.

Get a grip!

She took a deep breath and then cast a critical eye over the map she'd just drawn. Sketchy. Imperfect. But if it helped Peter, then it would have been worth it.

Rowan shot a quick glance at the other two. Olive was beaming at her. Her friend looked impressed – but frankly, that didn't mean anything. Olive Martinelli was the most loyal cheerleader anyone could wish for. She looked at Peter, but he was proving decidedly more difficult to read.

Rowan swallowed – annoyed with herself for just

how much she wanted him to like her stupid doodle. But that smile was definitely getting wider – which had to be a good sign, right? Maybe the map had helped?

Glancing back down at the drawing, Rowan's eyes traced the sketchy lines of the little cottages around the conference centre. It was the one bit of the map she hadn't added many details to, but then the entire place needed a lot of work, so she didn't feel too bad about taking a bit of creative licence where they were concerned!

'Erm... you've forgotten to add any sharks!' said Olive.

'Wait – what?!' said Peter.

'Don't worry – she's pulling your leg,' said Rowan, rolling her eyes at Olive. 'It's just one of Mr Harris's little obsessions!'

'Ah. Right!' said Peter, clearly relieved that he didn't have to work out how to get over the hurdle of enticing unsuspecting tourists to a tiny, windswept island that also had the added annoyance of killer sharks. 'Now then... where's my notepad,' he muttered, scuttling over to the bar to rummage through his bag.

Rowan watched as he hurried back over to the table, pulled up a chair and started leafing through his pad, bypassing page after page of scribbled-out notes until he finally found a fresh sheet.

'Right,' he said at last, writing the word *Crumcarey* in large, clear letters across the top as though, this time, he meant business. 'I know the perfect thing to open the guide with!'

'You do?' said Rowan, raising her eyebrows.

'Yep,' he said, looking her straight in the eye, which promptly made the back of her neck prickle. 'With the map you've just drawn!'

'That's a brilliant idea!' exclaimed Olive, dropping into the seat next to him.

'Oh, no,' said Rowan, a shot of pure horror coursing through her. 'That's a terrible idea. I mean, come on! I didn't spend any time doing it – it's really messy – just a sketch to help you get your bearings.'

She felt like he'd just knocked the breath right back out of her, and she crossed her arms, seeking a tiny bit of comfort from the gesture. Yes, the map might be fairly accurate - but she'd just grabbed the first things that had come to hand out of Olive's pencil case. She'd only done it because she'd been *forced to!*

'It's perfect!' said Peter.

For the first time since she'd met him, Rowan felt herself pinned by the full wattage of Peter's beaming smile. It did absolutely nothing to help with the whole *getting oxygen into her lungs* issue she was having.

'No – it's not,' said Rowan, frowning and staring down at her hastily scribbled drawing. She was having to resist the urge to grab the sheet of paper and scrunch it into a ball!

'Ohhh!' breathed Peter, his eyes growing wide. 'I've got an even better idea – you could illustrate the entire thing!' He gave a little clap, making Olive jump. 'We could have full-page drawings and paintings to go with the text, and then little details like this to break up the words!' He pointed from the puffins to the standing stones.

Rowan shivered. She *hated* this. He couldn't just spring something like this on her.

'Seriously,' said Peter, looking at Olive in excitement. 'I've been doing this for ages and normally I'd be taking photos of everything. I mean, I've got the gear with me... but I promise you, the work of a local artist will be so much more compelling and evocative than any photograph I could take.'

'I'm not an artist,' said Rowan, feeling the usual tightening heat in the back of her throat as she said it. She'd turned her back on all that nonsense years ago.

'Don't ever let me hear you say that again, young lady!' said Olive, crossing her arms. 'I don't think I know of a single other person who could pick up a knackered old pencil and do what you just did.'

'You're remarkable!' agreed Peter.

Rowan gave an uncomfortable squirm. This whole thing was meant to be about Crumcarey, not her. Sure, she'd drawn and painted every inch of the island many times over when she'd been growing up, spending hours lying on her belly, staring out over cliff edges and capturing the sea and birds and animals and clouds and everything that made her home special.

Charcoal, coloured pencils, Bic biros... if it made a

mark, she'd used it. Of course, watercolours had become her firm favourites after her dad had given her a set for her birthday one year. Hours would disappear in swirls of colour. Connor had regularly been sent out on his bike by their long-suffering parents to hunt her down and bring her back for tea. Still... she'd never once harboured any idea of doing it for a living though. At least, not since-

'You should have seen her when she was younger,' Olive said to an excited Peter, 'she always had a pencil or paintbrush in her hand. She did painting after painting. We were always having to order more paper in specially!'

'Are any of them still around?' said Peter, his eyes wide.

'No,' said Rowan

The word had just slipped out without any warning - but of course, it was a complete lie. Connor had told her that he'd saved a whole box of the bloody things and had them squirrelled away somewhere in his cottage. He'd kept them all these years and was planning on framing them when he got a chance. According to him, he wanted one hanging in every room the minute he'd finished doing the place up.

'At least... I don't think so,' she added in a mutter, not wanting to get caught out in a downright lie.

'Of course there are, silly!' said Olive.

'Really?!' said Peter. 'Because if there are, it would be great to have a look. We might be able to include them too. This is going to be amazing! I'm going to have to call my editor, of course, but I think she's going to go weak at the knees when she sees your work, Rowan!'

He was so excited now, that he'd sprung to his feet, looking like he wanted to rush to do something, if only he knew what!

'Well, she'd be a fool not to,' said Olive, staunchly. 'You know, I think there might still be a couple of Rowan's early pieces hanging over on the wall by the fireplace if we go down a layer or two! And I *know* there are some up in the bedrooms because I got them framed up specially.'

Rowan clenched her teeth. This could *not* be happening! Hell, she already had a career – she didn't *want* her old doodles to be in some stupid guidebook!

Rowan glared across the bar to where Olive was now pointing out various bits of island history to Peter – all pinned up on the far wall in a glorious mismatch of photos, cuttings and goodness knows what else.

She desperately wanted to say something to stop this nonsense in its tracks, but what was the point? For one thing, it didn't look like either Peter or Olive wanted to hear excuses right now, no matter how valid they were. And for another… well, she wasn't completely certain she still had a career, was she?! All she knew for sure was that there was one extremely angry boss back in the office in Edinburgh. Any moment now, the news might come in that she was officially unemployed.

Rowan let out a low groan and made her way across the bar to join the other two. She needed to keep a close eye on Olive, otherwise she'd probably find herself signed up to a ten-book contract before she knew what was happening!

CHAPTER 15

PETER

'Here's one!' said Olive, shifting aside a strand of bunting featuring some wonkily stitched thistle flowers.

Peter moved closer, and it was all he could do to stop his mouth from dropping open. He'd thought the map was a thing of beauty... but this... this was something else entirely.

'You did this?' he said, without turning around to look at Rowan.

'She did,' said Olive.

'I mean... I've never seen watercolours used like this before. It's so... alive!'

'It's just some cliffs with a few Fulmars messing around!' said Rowan.

Peter turned to her and was surprised to find her looking decidedly uncomfortable.

'Don't you like it?' he asked in surprise.

Rowan shrugged. 'I've never really thought about it before… it's just a painting.'

Peter shook his head. Didn't she understand how gifted she was? And as for the painting being hidden behind a scrappy bit of bunting on what looked to be the community notice board – well, it was practically a crime!

'This one's definitely got to go in the book!' said Peter. 'I'm assuming it's somewhere here on the island?' he added hastily.

'Of course,' said Olive. 'It's Craigie Head.'

'Amazing!'

He knew he was starting to sound ever so slightly insane – like a teenybopper having a total fan-boy moment, but he simply didn't care. This painting was quite literally breathtaking.

'Are there more?' he asked, turning to Olive.

She grinned at him and nodded.

Ten minutes later, after shifting various frames, maps, photographs and flags, Peter had helped Olive to uncover at least a dozen more of Rowan's paintings – all hanging in the same haphazard manner. Most of them were either blu-tacked to the wall or held up by ancient, slightly rusty drawing pins.

'I had no idea you had so many,' said Rowan.

She'd perched on a chair a little way away and had been strangely quiet and reserved while they'd been rummaging around on the wall. Peter couldn't quite understand it. Hopefully, he'd have the chance to get to the bottom of the whole thing later – maybe she was just feeling a bit overwhelmed by the sudden attention.

'You know, at this rate, I'm not going to need to supplement these with any photos at all!' said Peter. 'And you said there are more upstairs?' he asked, turning to Olive.

She nodded. 'You can pop up there and have a look around if you'd like.'

'I will,' said Peter, 'thanks. Blimey, these are so good it's hardly going to matter what I write next to them… people will just love them!'

Rowan coughed behind him, and he turned to her.

'Sorry,' he laughed. 'You probably thinking I'm being a total prat!'

'Of course I don't,' said Rowan, shaking her head and looking surprised. 'I'm just… not used to hearing anyone talk about my work, that's all.'

Her voice sounded flat, like she'd lost the bounce that had been there earlier when they'd been out on their magical mystery tour.

'I feel like I kind of recognise this one…' said Peter, pointing at the last painting they'd uncovered.

'That's Connor's place on The Dot!' said Olive.

'We drove past it earlier,' said Rowan, coming to stand next to him. 'Of course, it's got a roof now… not just a wall next to a random pile of stones!'

'Blimey!' said Peter. 'That must have taken him ages!'

'That's my brother for you,' said Rowan with a soft

laugh. 'He gets an idea in his head, and then there's no stopping him.'

'Sounds like someone else I know!' said Olive.

Peter watched as Rowan scuffed her toe awkwardly into the carpet.

'Not so much at the moment... but I'll figure it out,' she said.

'Do you paint much now?' he asked with interest.

Rowan's face fell even further as she gave her head a stiff little shake. 'Nope. Not my thing anymore. Olive... do you mind if I grab another coffee?'

'Go for it,' said Olive gently, and Rowan beat a hasty retreat.

'Was it something I said?' asked Peter in a low voice.

He couldn't understand what was going on, but there was definitely something he was missing. Why had Rowan's entire demeanour changed so drastically? It was like she'd caved in on herself somehow - he couldn't understand it.

'It's not you,' said Olive quietly. 'But it's not my place to say, either. I'm sure she'll tell you when she's ready. Just... tread a bit lightly while she wraps her head around things a bit, maybe?'

'Okay,' said Peter, nodding quickly. 'I will. Thanks.'

The last thing he wanted to do was spook her and lose the chance of showcasing her beautiful work. But... if Rowan wasn't up for it, he'd have to respect that decision.

'Would you mind if I take a peep upstairs now... maybe give her a chance for a breather?' he asked.

'Sure. Come on, I'll take you up,' said Olive. 'This place is a total maze... we'll have to send out a search party if you go alone!'

∽

Ten minutes later, they were back in the bar, and Peter's mind was officially blown... mainly by the array of Rowan's gorgeous work that was displayed in the guest rooms, but also because the Tallyaff's bedrooms were stunning. That was the only word for it. Its rather grey and dour exterior hid the most luxurious accommodation he could imagine.

'I can't wait to write about this place for the book!' said Peter. 'Next time I come and visit, I'm booking in with you.'

'Ah, get away with you,' said Olive, though she was beaming at him as she said it, clearly chuffed with the compliment. 'Anyway, I'm happy to hear you're already planning a return trip.'

Peter returned her smile, surprised to realise that this was true too. Yesterday, he'd been ready to escape at the earliest opportunity, provided he never had to get back on that flying tin can again! Today, however, Crumcarey had him officially intrigued. He hadn't even scratched the surface of the little island yet. He couldn't wait to start exploring some of Rowan's favourite places… that's if he hadn't completely freaked her out, of course!

'Hi!' he said, spotting Rowan who was sitting at the bar, leafing through a magazine as she nibbled at yet another pastry.

'Hey,' she said. 'Any luck?'

'Of course!' laughed Olive. 'I told you I'd had some of your pieces framed.'

'I think we could use most of them,' said Peter, 'but I'm not sure there's quite enough for the whole guide…' he paused.

He really wanted to ask her if she'd be willing to paint some new pieces, especially when they'd decided on the points of interest they wanted to include. But, after Olive's warning, he had a feeling that might wipe the tentative smile on Rowan's face straight back off again.

'Well…' said Rowan, 'I've been thinking and I'm pretty sure Connor said he's got a box of them stashed in the cottage somewhere.'

Peter bit his tongue to stop himself from squeaking in excitement.

'We could have a look if you'd like?' she said. 'I wanted to throw them all away when I moved to Edinburgh, but he hoarded most of them, I think.'

'Thank god!' said Peter in horror. The words slipped out before he had the chance to stop them, and he clapped his hand over his mouth for a second. 'Sorry… I mean… that would have been so sad!'

'You've not seen them yet,' said Rowan, her face serious. 'Trust me, they don't all deserve a spot on a wall... or in a book, come to that. They're mostly just the random daubings of a bored teenager.'

Somehow, Peter highly doubted that. He caught Olive's eye, and the little shake of her head accompanied by a subtle widening of her eyes told him that his hunch was probably right.

'Well... if you don't mind me checking them out,' he said carefully, 'it would give me a great starting place to see what else we need to pull together.'

He still wanted to ask her if she'd be willing to paint some updated scenes or add to those that were already available, but he was sensing that right now, that would be majorly jumping the gun... especially considering he hadn't even asked her if she was willing to go ahead with all this. He'd need to call Mel, of course, but first...

'Rowan, before I take this up with my editor... if she's up for it, are you willing to have your work included?'

There, that sounded broad enough. They could work out the logistics of how it all might work after he'd got the go-ahead from Mel. Something was telling him that his editor would jump at his proposal the moment she caught sight of Rowan's work... but first, he needed Rowan to agree, otherwise, there was no point taking this any further.

Rowan was nibbling at a fingernail, clearly thinking hard.

'Okay,' she said eventually. 'If you think it'll help Crumcarey, then I guess it's fine to include some of them. As long as I get the final say if I really don't want you to use a piece.'

'Good girl!' said Olive, smiling at her approvingly.

'Brilliant!' said Peter, doing his best to keep his voice calm and steady. 'And that's totally fair. Erm... right... in that case, I could do with speaking to my editor before we dig into things any further!'

'Sure!' said Olive, practically bopping up and down with excitement. 'Why don't you come through to the back with me. You can use the landline in my office – you'll be lucky to find any mobile signal around here, and it would probably only last you about thirty seconds if you did find a patch!'

'Perfect,' said Peter, 'thanks. And you're sure?' he said, turning back to Rowan.

He knew he shouldn't be pushing his luck by asking her a second time. But he wanted her to be all in – and he wanted her to feel like this was her decision rather than feeling forced into the whole thing just because he was so excited by the idea.

'I'm sure,' said Rowan. Her voice was tight, but she was nodding.

'Cool,' said Peter.

Okay, so she didn't exactly sound excited – not like most people would be at the thought of their artwork being published for the first time - but at least she was a little more certain about the whole thing. He'd take that, for now!

'Right... let's see if Mel will give us the go-ahead. Then maybe we can head over to the cottage and hunt for the other paintings?'

'Sounds like a plan,' said Rowan, shooting him a small smile.

Peter felt his toes curl. In that moment, he realised that he'd do pretty much anything to keep earning those smiles.

CHAPTER 16

ROWAN

Rowan watched Olive lead Peter behind the bar and out through the kitchen towards her little office. The moment they were out of sight, she slumped forwards, buried her head in her hands and let out a frustrated little growl. She'd prefer to be screaming at the sea right now, but if she did that it would be around the island in seconds that she'd completely lost the plot.

Resting her forehead on the soft arm of her jumper, she blinked into the cocoon of darkness. Why on earth was she being such a weirdo about all this? Poor Peter – he was like a kid in a sweetshop and she knew she should be over the moon at his reaction to her work. It wasn't every day someone told you they wanted to work with you on a book, was it?

Rowan let out a long sigh followed by another little groan. The thing was, those paintings felt like they belonged to another lifetime... another person, even. They came from a period when she'd been so happy, content and safe on her island home, with the love of her family surrounding her. Her mum and dad and Connor – all on her side.

Rowan hadn't felt like that in years... and she hadn't painted in years either. It was something that belonged to the past, and she wasn't sure she wanted to wake up the ghosts.

But then, who was she to say no? If it helped Crumcarey come back to life, any amount of discomfort would be worth it. Everyone else on the island had made it quite clear they'd do almost anything to help - including inventing cinemas and lama petting zoos! Here she was with an easy fix at her fingertips – something the others would probably give their right arms for – and yet she'd just come very close to being a completely selfish a-hole. That's what had forced her to agree, even though the thought of it made her want to leg it back to Edinburgh without another word.

'You okay there?'

Rowan sat bolt upright, blinking away the moisture that had crept into her eyes.

'Yup!' she nodded quickly, rubbing her face hard. 'Yup – just...'

'It's okay,' said Olive gently. 'I get it.'

Rowan gave an awkward shrug. She wasn't sure if her friend *really* understood what was at the root of her weirdness. Hell, she wasn't sure anyone did... maybe Connor... but he wasn't here.

'Do you really think my paintings could make a difference?' she asked, doing her best to keep her voice calm and level. 'Do you think they might help get the guidebook out there?'

Olive considered for a moment. 'I think the guidebook will happen whether you agree to Peter using your work or not. After all, he's come willing and prepared to do photographs.'

Rowan let out a sigh of relief. There – straight from the horse's mouth. It wouldn't matter what she decided. She wasn't going to ruin anything if she asked Peter not to use her work after all.

'But-' said Olive.

Damnit! Why was there always a "but"?!

'But... I think your work could make it something really special. I don't know for sure, obviously, but something tells me your paintings would put that book into the right hands and bring us the visitors Crumcarey really deserves... because it would have a bit of your spirit in there too. A bit of the true spirit of the island.'

Anything that made the straight-talking Olive Martinelli start speaking in near-mystical tones had to be serious.

Rowan gave a tight nod. 'If all he needs are the ones you and Connor have saved, I guess I'll be fine with it,' she said. 'But I don't think I can do any new ones for him… not now.'

Olive gazed at her for a long moment, and Rowan felt a heavy weight settle on her shoulders.

'You want my advice?' said Olive.

Rowan nodded.

'Don't go worrying about it until you know more,' said Olive. 'This Mel person might not like the idea. Peter might just be getting ahead of himself in his excitement. It might not be his call to make, so there's no point getting yourself all twisted up about it until there's an actual decision to be made.'

Rowan nodded again. It was a good point… but weirdly, the idea of Peter getting a "no" from his editor made her feel even more wretched. The poor guy was so excited about his plan, he'd be crushed!

'Yeah – you're right,' she said when she noticed that Olive was still watching her closely.

'You take him over to The Dot and have a look for those other paintings today – but then, get on with showing him around and enjoy the island a bit. Forget about all this until you hear back!'

'Right,' said Rowan, squaring her shoulders. 'Yes. You're right.'

'And make sure he's taking photos of everything as he goes,' said Olive. 'Just in case.'

Just in case Mel said no. Just in case Mel said yes but she, Rowan, decided that her answer was a no after all.

'Right!' said Rowan again. She sat up properly and did her best to push it all to the back of her mind for a moment. 'Well... in that case, I've got a major favour to ask.'

Olive narrowed her eyes. 'Oh yes?'

'I've eaten Connor's cottage bare... any chance I can grab some shopping on my tab? If I'm going to feed Peter this evening, I don't think he'd fancy sharing my last two soggy cream crackers!'

Rowan knew she should be ashamed - having to scrounge because of her anaemic bank account – but frankly, it wasn't entirely her fault. She'd not been expecting company - and she'd been doing fairly well living off Connor's store cupboards until now.

'Of course,' said Olive. 'Anything for the new artist of Crumcarey!'

'Thanks!' said Rowan, feeling her entire body squeeze with apprehension. If Olive carried on like that, the whole thing would be all over the island in hours, and then the decision would be out of her hands either way. It was always the way. Need help? They'd all be there. Any gossip? They'd all know.

'Thanks. And... can we keep that bit to ourselves?' said Rowan in a low, pleading voice. 'About the art stuff?'

'Good luck with that,' laughed Olive, nodding over at the door where Mr Harris had just appeared with McGregor.

'Oh noooo!' sighed Rowan.

Olive grinned at her and shrugged.

'There should be a warning on the opening page of the book, if you ask me,' said Rowan, clambering to her feet and returning Mr Harris's salute.

'What's that?' asked Olive, already busying herself with his drink.

'Welcome to Crumcarey – the place where secrets go to die!'

'Catchy... but not quite the tone we're going for,' chuckled Olive, before setting the steam spout whistling.

'Hullo!' said Mr Harris, plonking himself down onto Rowan's stool.

'Hi, Mr Harris... how are the lamas?' she asked, bending to let McGregor give the back of her hand a nervy, tentative sniff before he promptly leant back into her shins with a crash, demanding ear-scratches.

'On their way, lass,' said Mr Harris, 'but if your writer laddie would like a tour of their barn, just bring him along.'

'I will,' she chuckled. 'Right, I'll start getting some bits and pieces from the shop. Olive, can I grab your order pad so I can make a list?'

Olive placed Mr Harris's coffee down on the bar and waved her hand dismissively. 'Don't worry about that. I'd only have to feed him if you didn't. Help yourself!'

Rowan knew that it was Olive's way of making sure she didn't feel too bad about scrounging food, but right now, the customary kindness meant more to her than ever.

Quickly stammering her thanks, she hurried away towards the shop before the other two could spot the tears that had just sprung to her eyes.

Rowan grabbed a basket and scuttled between the shelves, pretending to be staring intently at the rows of tinned food while she did her best to pull herself together.

Urgh! Today was turning into one of *those* days. She should have just insisted on borrowing one of the OS maps Olive kept for her visitors instead of agreeing to draw one. That's what started all this mess. It had just opened a can of worms - and she'd been doing surprisingly well at keeping the ghosts of the past firmly in their place, too. Now it felt like she'd cracked the lid open and they were swirling around her, threatening to remind her just how much she'd lost when she'd left the island.

But no – that wasn't right. Rowan had lost those things *before* she'd left Crumcarey behind her. She'd left *because* she'd lost so much - and she simply couldn't bear to be reminded of it every single day…

Rowan let out a long breath. She needed to forget about all that and just focus on the job in hand. First things first – she needed to feed Peter… and to do that, she needed to shop. Reaching out, she snagged a bag of pasta from the shelf and tossed it into her basket.

'Well, it's a start,' she sighed.

CHAPTER 17

PETER

'How's my favourite writer?' Mel's voice boomed down the line. 'Soaked to the skin and eaten alive yet?'

'Thank heavens you don't do the guidebook intros!' laughed Peter.

He heard Mel chuckle.

'Nah – that's what I've got you for, old man! Anyway, what can I do you for... and if you've called to beg to be allowed home early, the answer's a big fat no!'

'Nope, not that,' said Peter, wondering – not for the first time – if Mel was a bit of a mind reader. 'I might have begged you about twelve hours ago when the wind was threatening to blow me home without the help of a plane anyway... but the sun's out today. Makes quite a difference, you know!'

'I'll take your word for it,' said Mel. 'Anyway – if

you're not begging for an extraction package, what's up? The locals giving you problems?'

'Funny you should say that,' said Peter. 'It looks like they've all got wind of my arrival. All sorts of weird little pop-up businesses have appeared. It made my first tour around the island... interesting.'

'When you say *pop-up businesses*, give me an example here,' said Mel.

'Lama Cuddling and Petting Zoo?' said Peter.

'Ooh, that would be brilliant for the book!' said Mel.

'Yeah... only there aren't any lamas as far as I can tell,' he said. 'I think you need to drop all notions of the cute, city pop-ups you've seen before!'

'I've been to goat yoga,' said Mel. 'It was fun! I had one on my back during downward dog. Not sure it helped with the stretching, and it did eat some of my hair... but it was definitely a talking point!'

Peter snorted, doing his best to rid himself of the mental image of his tweedy editor doing yoga in her pearls with a goat balanced on her back.

'I promise it's nothing like that!' he said. 'Most of them are cafés that are just people's front rooms with an instant coffee available, and the museum is a barn full of junk.'

'And you've seen these for yourself?' said Mel.

'Well no... but Rowan, my guide, told me,' said Peter.

'You'd better make sure,' said Mel. 'A section on local colour might be a nice little addition.'

'Hm,' said Peter sceptically.

What was the point of using a local guide if you didn't listen to them? He knew that if there was *anything* good to see on the island, Rowan would make sure he saw it. But they were getting right off-topic, and he was desperate to get to the real point for calling before Mel pulled her usual disappearing act and hung up before he'd even pitched his idea.

'I'll think about it,' he said. 'But now you mention it, there *is* something a bit different I want to include.'

'Different?' said Mel, the laughter disappearing from her voice. 'You know that's like a rude word in publishing, right? We all say we want the "new thing" but what we really want is nice and ordinary. Tried and tested, you know?'

'I know,' said Peter, raising an eyebrow.

Oh yes – he knew that all too well. He had two entire boxes of book proposals sitting in the flat, filled to the brim with ideas that were just a little bit *too* different for publishers.

'But I think you'll like this one,' he said quickly, sensing he was losing his audience. 'In fact, you've mentioned it's something you're looking for anyway...'

'Okay – I'm listening,' said Mel.

'I've found a local artist... and she's amazing,' said Peter.

'Oh?' said Mel. 'What kind of amazing? The kind where you promise her the world and a shot in publishing because you fancy her?'

Peter cringed. Bloody hell, he'd forgotten just how ruthless Mel could be when she was guarding the company's purse strings! It didn't help that once again, she was a bit too close to the truth for comfort.

'The kind that is an undiscovered genius,' said Peter steadily. He knew he needed to use language she'd understand if this had any chance of working. 'The kind that will sell books.'

∽

Peter followed the narrow passageway that led back to the bar of the Tallyaff.

'All sorted?' called Olive, the moment he reappeared.

Peter smiled and nodded. Olive was standing with an elderly gent at the far end of the bar, and something told him that he needed to talk to Rowan alone first... and maybe Olive second... but definitely not anyone else until things really *were* sorted. In publishing, that was something that could take a ridiculous amount of time to achieve!

'Where's Rowan?' he asked.

'Over in the shop,' said Olive.

'Perfect! Thanks,' said Peter, hurrying out from behind the bar and heading straight over there. He was pretty sure Olive had been about to introduce him to the other customer, but he'd just have to apologise later.

'Hey!' he said, rounding the corner, only to find Rowan staring absently at a chiller cabinet. She had a basket resting against her hip but so far, there was just a solitary bag of pasta in there.

'Hi!' she said, turning to him with an uncertain smile. 'Everything... okay?'

Peter nodded. 'All good. Mel was interested to see your work.'

'Oh... okay, great!' said Rowan.

'Look, I may as well tell you, trying to get them to do anything out of the ordinary is... difficult,' he said. He might as well be completely straight with her. 'It might not come to anything. And... well, I'm sorry – I got so excited seeing your work, and I do think there's a good chance they'll go for it because it's a direction Mel has been considering for ages but...'

'Don't get my hopes up?' said Rowan, giving him a huge smile.

'You look weirdly happy at the idea that it might not work out,' laughed Peter. Normally this would have people gutted and nervous, but it seemed to have brought her back to life.

Rowan shrugged. 'Just gives us the chance to explore the island while we're waiting, right?'

'Sounds like a plan,' said Peter, 'though I would still like to take a look at the other paintings first if that's okay with you? Mel wants me to send some through to her, so it would be great to have the full selection to choose from.'

Rowan frowned and then nodded. 'Sure. That makes sense.'

'Only thing is, I don't have any signal here and there's no wifi at the cottage,' said Peter.

'That's easy enough,' said Rowan. 'We can just ask Olive if she'd mind uploading the photos for you. I think she's got some weird plugin that gives her steady internet.'

'Good call,' said Peter. 'I guess we can take photos of everything on my phone and then reconvene here in the morning to send them to Mel?'

Rowan nodded. 'Now... onto more important stuff... what do you want to eat?!'

Peter laughed. 'Well, we've got a lot of work to do... so...'

'I got as far as pasta,' she said, lifting her basket. 'Then I started to double-guess myself. What if you don't like pasta. What if you're intolerant to something. What if-'

'Pasta's a great idea!' said Peter, deciding to let her off the hook. 'And I can whip up a tomato sauce to go with it if you like?'

'I'm loving the sound of that,' said Rowan, an easy smile back on her face. She was clearly much happier now that they were off the sticky topic of her artwork.

'Okay,' said Peter, 'so I'll need some tomatoes, mixed herbs, puree, onions... salt, pepper...' he whirled around the little space, tossing ingredients into the basket as he went. Then he started adding extras like olives, crusty rolls and spicy nuts.

'Is it a wine kind of day?' he asked, staring at the impressive selection.

'Normally, I would definitely say yes,' said Rowan with a grin. 'But I'm playing taxi driver today, and I definitely want to get you back to Groatie Buckie Cottage in one piece. So, not for me - but don't let me stop you if you'd like a glass!'

'Nah!' said Peter, 'let's grab a bottle of this instead.'

He grabbed a bottle of pink, non-alcoholic fizz. He really wasn't sure why, given the fact that Mel's dire warnings were still ringing in his ears, but he was in the mood to celebrate.

'Chocolate?' he added.

'Better not,' sighed Rowan. 'Erm... Olive's footing the bill for this lot, so I don't want to take the mic!'

'No chance,' he said, shaking his head. I'm paying!'

'But-'

'No buts!' said Peter, noticing that she had that worried look on her face again. 'I get expenses on these trips. I think my company can foot the bill for a nice meal and a decent bit of comfort food after they switched me from the tropics to Crumcarey.'

'Okay – you've got a deal,' said Rowan. 'In that case... what's your poison? Milk? White? Delicious and dark?'

Peter grinned at her and checked out the huge chocolate selection. 'I don't know about you,' he said slowly, 'but I've always been a quantity kind of guy when it comes to chocolate.'

'Me too!' laughed Rowan. 'Keep your fancy single-wrapped truffles, I want a bar that you can barely fit in through the front door.'

'Well… that definitely narrows it down then!' he said.

They both reached out and grabbed either end of a massive, royal-purple-wrapped slab of chocolate.

'Bingo!' laughed Rowan, taking it from him before trying - and failing - to fit it in the basket. 'Actually, here – you carry this,' she said thrusting it back at him and then adding a pack of coffee and some milk to the basket. 'I wish I had a nice big expense account with my stupid job!'

'Are you really not an artist?' said Peter.

He instantly wanted to stuff his fist in his mouth. Rowan's face had clouded over and she shook her head, her dark hair quivering under the strip light.

Quick! Think of something to change the subject!

'So… what *do* you do? Must be nice if they let you have the summer off to spend back here.'

Smooth, Peter!

The hole he'd just dug himself was getting deeper - he could tell by the nervous, slightly hunted expression that had just flitted across her face.

'You don't have to-'

'Shh,' she said, flicking her eyes over to where Mr Harris and Olive were still deep in conversation.

'Sorry, you don't need to tell me,' said Peter quickly, 'I was just being nosy.'

'It's fine... but not in here?' she nodded at the other two. 'I'll fill you in in the car?'

'Of course,' he said, a little ripple of relief going through him.

'And if we're doing that, I'm going to need these,' she said, adding two bars of Turkish Delight to their basket.

CHAPTER 18

ROWAN

Urgh, what was it with this man? He seemed to have an uncanny knack for blundering right into her best-kept secrets and strange insecurities. Now she was going to be stuck in a car with him and have to tell him about her stupid job and her stupid boss and her stupid gardening leave. Balls.

She sighed and stood back to watch as Peter and Olive went head-to-head about the grocery bill. Or, at least, that's what *Peter* thought was happening.

'No,' said Olive. 'No, you mustn't pay!'

Rowan bit her lip, doing her best not to laugh. It was the most half-hearted protest she'd ever heard.

'Don't argue, Olive,' said Peter, 'or I'll give you a bad write-up!'

Olive snorted at that. 'Fine, you win,' she said, promptly grabbing her card machine and keying in the amount. When she told him the total, Rowan's eyes practically started to water. Blimey – that would have drained her bank account dry – and then she really would have been screwed!

'Anyway,' said Peter, 'I've got a favour I need to beg before we head off.'

'Oh yes,' said Olive.

'If I pop back in the morning with photos of any more paintings we find at Connor's cottage, could I use your internet to send them through to my editor?'

'Sure - I've got a computer you can use. The internet's a bit slow, though... it's one of those wired connections,' said Olive.

'Thanks, that's brilliant,' said Peter. 'It's just so that Mel can take a look and then show the rest of the company if she wants to take it further.'

'She's an idiot if she doesn't,' said Olive stoutly.

'Hardly,' laughed Rowan.

She was grateful for Olive's never-ending support, but this wasn't Crumcarey's newsletter they were talking about here – it was a book. Rowan was under no illusions - she knew her paintings weren't up to scratch, even if the other two were having all these ridiculous notions.

'Well, we'll see,' said Olive in an ominous tone.

Rowan quickly made a mental note to warn Peter about keeping Olive away from any direct contact with his editor at all costs, otherwise the woman would find herself with a lot of unwanted "encouragement".

'Right!' said Rowan, clapping her hands and making the other two jump, 'let's get this show on the road.'

'Have fun!' beamed Olive, giving Rowan a huge wink, promptly making her blush for precisely no reason. She quickly grabbed one of the three laden carrier bags in a bid to hide her flushed cheeks

'See you tomorrow,' she said.

'Bye Olive,' said Peter. 'Thanks!'

Rowan hurried to the car park with her head down. The minute she stepped out into the soft early afternoon air, she let out a long sigh, as though she'd been holding her breath.

'You okay?' said Peter lightly, as he waited for her to open the boot of her car so that they could stash their shopping inside.

'Yeah, fine,' said Rowan, shooting him a rueful grin. 'It's been quite a day, that's all.'

Peter nodded but didn't say anything else and she was grateful. She needed to get on the road and away from the Tallyaff. She adored Olive but being in there could feel a bit like being in a fishbowl... though why she should feel like that today was beyond her. It was far too quiet - especially for this time of year.

A spike of unease went through her. Maybe Olive had been right... maybe Crumcarey really *was* in more trouble than she'd realised. This book of Peter's had to be a success!

The pair of them were quiet as she pulled out of the carpark. Rowan was grateful. She felt like she needed a few moments of peace to get her head around everything. As they whizzed past three pop-up cafes in a row, she let out a sigh.

'You know,' said Peter, 'Mel actually wants me to go and check out Mr Harris's petting zoo!'

'Why on earth would she want you to do that?' laughed Rowan in surprise, glad to be yanked out of her spiralling thoughts.

'Well, what you need to understand about Mel is that she's the kind of person who pays several hundred pounds to do yoga sessions with goats jumping all over her!' said Peter, rolling his eyes.

'Hey! Goat yoga is awesome!' said Rowan.

'You are kidding me, right?' said Peter, turning to her with mock horror on his face. 'You and the goats?!'

'Yes. And I'm not ashamed,' chuckled Rowan, tilting her chin defiantly. 'They were super-cute and distracted me nicely from the fact that I have the balance of a… of a…'

'Not very balance-y thing?' said Peter.

'Precisely,' said Rowan with a nod. 'Besides, goat yoga was definitely the best of the bunch when it came to the terrible team-building exercises work sent us on.'

The sentence hung in the car like a levitating stone. *Whhhhy?!* She'd clearly made a pact with herself to make today as awkward as humanly possible. There had been zero need to mention work. Peter hadn't asked again, had he? He might have forgotten all about it if she'd just kept her stupid mouth shut.

'You're lucky,' said Peter. 'My lot never cough up for anything like that.'

'To be fair, I'd swap my goats for your expense allowance!' said Rowan.

'So... now we're out of the Tallyaff... can I ask where you work?' said Peter, clearly intrigued.

Rowan shot him a quick look, only to find him peering at her with interest. She grinned at him, she couldn't help it. 'Don't get all excited. I'm not some kind of spy or codebreaker... or a stripper!'

Peter spluttered. 'I never... I mean, I didn't... just you said...'

Rowan was laughing properly now. 'Calm down!'

'It's just,' said Peter, still spluttering, 'you looked so uncomfortable when I asked you in the shop!'

'That's because anything you say in the shop is around the island in seconds,' said Rowan.

'But... there was no one there other than that old man and Olive,' said Peter.

'That "old man" is the famous Mr Harris, I'll have you know,' said Rowan, realising with a certain amount of horror that she hadn't done the polite thing and introduced the pair of them.

'That's the owner of the petting zoo?' said Peter.

'No Peter,' said Rowan, indicating to pull over into a passing place at the side of the road, 'that's the owner of several large, empty barns and a herd of Scotland's most pampered cows.'

'Right, right. I keep thinking that if I wish hard enough for lamas, they might come true!' he said, smiling. 'Anyway, it was just the two of them and me... surely...?'

Rowan shook her head as she killed the engine. 'I'm not quite sure how the Crumcarey jungle drums work, but there's definitely some kind of witchcraft at work. Say anything in that shop – it doesn't matter if the place is completely deserted and you're talking to yourself – and it's right around the island in seconds!'

'Right, and you don't want everyone to know that you're a spy,' said Peter, grinning at her. '*Not* a stripper!'

Rowan elbowed him in the ribs, before realising it was probably not a very professional thing to do. He didn't look like he minded much.

'So... are you going to fill me in?' he asked. 'And... why exactly have we stopped? We're not at The Dot yet are we?'

Rowan shook her head. 'I will fill you in – but there's something way more exciting I want to do first!'

'O-kay,' said Peter, sounding unsure.

'Follow me!' said Rowan, jumping out of the car. She didn't wait to see if he was following her but headed straight over the grassy verge and down a sandy track towards the beach.

'Wait...' puffed Peter, catching her up, 'is that a...'

'An ice cream van?' laughed Rowan, turning to see a

look of wonder on his face. 'Yep, that is exactly what that is. That's Ruby.'

'But… it's on the beach… out of sight…' said Peter, shaking his head in confusion.

'It is,' said Rowan with a shrug.

'Another pop-up?' he asked.

'Nope. This is definitely one for your notebook!' said Rowan. 'I'm assuming I might be able to tempt you with a little pre-dinner snack?'

'Are you kidding me?!' said Peter looking delighted. 'If they've got coffee ice cream, I'm there!'

'Ohhh… you don't even know the meaning of coffee ice cream until you've tried some from Ruby,' said Rowan, feeling lighter than she had all day. Sod worrying about some idiot back in Edinburgh and what Peter might think when she told him the real reason she was loafing around Crumcarey for the summer.

'I'm confused,' said Peter as they drew nearer to the vintage van with its gorgeous white, cream and raspberry paintwork, 'is the van owned by someone called Ruby or-?'

'Nope. The van *is* Ruby. And she's owned by Frank and Stella,' she said. 'Stella is Olive's daughter,' she added.

'Ah!' said Peter. 'Right… good to know!'

'Rule number one of island life… everyone is related somehow! It makes dating practically impossible!' she chuckled.

'Is that why you moved to Edinburgh?' said Peter.

Rowan felt the joke as if it was a physical blow... but Peter wasn't to know the real reason she'd left Crumcarey behind her. She hadn't told him, and it definitely wasn't a conversation she wanted to have right now.

'I think I'm going for roasted strawberry and black pepper today!' she said cheerily, executing the clumsiest change of subject of her entire life.

'We wondered if we'd be seeing you two!'

A cheerful face appeared at Ruby's hatch, and Rowan grinned at Stella.

'This is-'

'Peter? Yeah, we know,' said Frank, his face appearing at Stella's shoulder.

'Erm... hi!' said Peter, looking a bit taken aback.

'What was I saying about those jungle drums?' laughed Rowan.

'Point taken!' said Peter nodding.

'Don't look so worried,' laughed Stella. 'We don't have any weird business suggestions so that we can get into that book of yours.'

'No – you guys are the rare ones who actually have a business,' said Rowan.

'Well, you've certainly got everyone in an uproar!' said Frank. 'We had Mr Harris here yesterday telling us all about your book and everyone's plans to "help"!' said Frank.

'I should have known it was Mr Harris behind the whole thing,' sighed Rowan, rolling her eyes.

'Yeah – he even offered us a pitch at the petting zoo,' said Stella. 'He said he could practically guarantee us a spot in the new guidebook that way! He said he had a long line of businesses who'd take his arm off for the opportunity, but he wanted to offer it to us first.'

'Well,' said Peter, 'from what we saw this morning, there are definitely plenty of new businesses.'

'Hmm... I bet,' said Stella. 'I think he just wanted a free strawberry ice cream, to be honest.'

'Cheeky bugger,' said Rowan. 'Though I have to approve of his flavour choice!'

'One for you too?' said Frank, grabbing a scoop.

'Please!' Rowan nodded. She could already feel her mouth watering in anticipation. 'And a coffee one for Peter?' she added, turning to him with her eyebrows raised in question.

'Yes please!' said Peter. 'Though we're not expecting any freebies! Ruby's got a spot in the guidebook anyway – she's gorgeous!'

'You get a freebie for the compliment!' grinned Stella. 'The thing that's really worrying me... no, maybe I shouldn't say...'

'Out with it, Stella,' said Rowan.

'Well,' she said awkwardly, 'we're just hoping things don't change too much, you know? I mean, I know the guidebook will bring in new visitors but... we just don't want to be run off our feet. We love it here just as it is.'

Rowan could see the look of mild surprise on

Peter's face as he turned to peer around him at the decidedly customer-free expanse of Big Sandy.

'Don't worry,' he said. 'It won't change too much. It might just mean that the visitors you *do* get are the right kind – ones that want to enjoy the peace and quiet – but at least they'll know where to come to find a delicious treat while they're doing it.'

Rowan shot him an approving smile, which he completely failed to return as he was too busy taking a huge bite of the heaped waffle cone Frank had just handed him.

'Well… that doesn't sound too bad then,' said Frank. 'Mr Harris was going on about cruise ships.'

Rowan snorted as she accepted her own ice cream. 'Yeah well… Mr Harris is adamant there are sharks, so…'

'Okay, point taken!' said Stella.

CHAPTER 19

PETER

*P*eter licked the last dribble of coffee ice cream from his fingers before letting himself back into Rowan's car. The minute he closed the door, it was like someone had hit the mute button. It might be beautiful and sunny out there right now, but the wind was getting back up again. What with that swirling around his head along with the persistent rush of the waves along Big Sandy, it was quite overwhelming.

He let out a long sigh.

'You okay?' laughed Rowan, shooting him a look.

'Still getting used to the wind!' he said, smiling at her.

'That's not wind!' laughed Rowan. 'That's a mere tickle. You wait until you visit in winter. I'll show you wind! There are days you can't even stand up outside –

it feels like it's going to turn your kneecaps inside out if you try it!'

'Sounds delightful!' laughed Peter.

'It's actually kind of nice,' said Rowan. 'You just curl up indoors and batten down the hatches. Though it tends to be a good plan to know where your candles are… and keeping the store cupboards stocked is essential!'

'Well, we've got enough ice cream to last us at least a couple of weeks!' said Peter, waving the little paper bag Stella had presented them with. Inside was a large tub of vanilla ice cream.

'On that note, shall we get going?' said Rowan.

'To The Dot?' said Peter.

'To The Dot!' cried Rowan with a cheer, pulling the little car neatly out of the parking spot and back onto the winding island road.

Peter stayed silent for a moment, staring out at the fields, dotted with wildflowers and contented-looking cows. Even though he'd been all over the world, with the sun out like it was now, he couldn't imagine anywhere on earth more beautiful than this.

'I can't imagine ever wanting to move away from here if this was home,' he said. 'You must miss it?'

Rowan nodded, staring fixedly ahead of her. 'I do,' she said in a quiet voice. 'But I've always loved city life… well, until recently…' she trailed off again.

Peter got the distinct feeling he was about to put his foot in it again if he carried on down this line of questioning. It was the last thing he wanted to do. Things had seemed so fun and easy between them down on the beach while they'd been chatting with Stella and Frank, and he was pretty keen to keep it that way.

'So... if you don't work for the MI5... what *is* it you do for a job?' he said, glancing at her. 'Though I'm still finding it hard to believe you're not a full-time artist!'

'I'm not an *any*-time artist!' said Rowan. 'I was being serious when I said I haven't picked up a brush in eleven years.'

'That's a very specific amount of time!' said Peter curiously.

'Yeah well...' she trailed off again and Peter bit his tongue. There was clearly some kind of big secret here that she really didn't want to tell him... and somehow he kept blundering towards it.

'Anyway!' she said, 'to answer your question, I work for a design agency.'

'Ah-ha!' said Peter. 'I knew you were an artist of some kind.'

'I'm in their accounts department,' said Rowan.

'What?!' said Peter incredulously. Somehow, he just hadn't pictured Rowan working with numbers.

'Don't look so horrified!' she laughed. 'I couldn't really figure out what I wanted to do with myself when I left home, so I trained up in accounts. Keeps me out of trouble... or at least, it used to.'

'Why?' said Peter – then promptly bit his tongue.

Rowan let out a long sigh. 'Promise you won't tell

anyone here?' she said. 'It's not that I don't trust them – I just don't want them turning up at my office with a bunch of pitchforks!'

'Okay,' said Peter, wondering what on earth she was about to tell him. 'Deal.'

'I've been suspended,' she said flatly. 'They called it "put on gardening leave" but frankly, that's bollocks, because people on gardening leave usually get paid.'

'But... what did you do?!' said Peter in surprise.

'Urgh... it's so embarrassing,' she sighed.

'What is?!'

'You know those team-building things we were talking about earlier?' she said.

'The goat yoga?' said Peter.

'Yeah,' she said.

'You didn't... steal a goat?' he said.

Rowan snorted and shook her head. 'Tempting, but no.' She let out a long sigh. 'I kneed another type of horny old goat in the balls.'

'What?!' said Peter, caught between horror and laughter. He turned in his seat slightly to stare at her. 'You don't mean literally?'

'I do,' said Rowan. 'My boss.'

'Shiiiit!' breathed Peter.

'Yeah. The thing the company didn't know was that he was also my boyfriend,' she sighed. 'Or at least, we'd been seeing each other. It was against company policy, so we kept it completely quiet.'

'Right,' said Peter. 'So... why the gooseberry crushing?' he said, doing his best not to cross his legs. 'Did he cheat on you?'

Rowan shook her head. Then nodded.

'No? Or yes?' said Peter. 'And you don't have to tell me if you don't want to – you don't even know me!'

'It's fine,' said Rowan, 'it's actually a bit of a relief if I'm honest.'

'Okay – so...?'

'Yes, he was cheating on me, as it happens,' said Rowan. 'Seems I thought it was more serious between us than Ben did. But that's not why I kneed him.'

'Really?' said Peter. 'I would have.'

'Yeah... but...' she paused, clearly stealing herself. 'He knew I was keen to try for a job in the creative side of the company. It's the first time I've let myself go anywhere near anything creative ever since...' she paused again. 'Since I left home. Anyway, he was the only person I told.'

'Right...?' said Peter.

'He was sweet and helpful, and suggested I put together a pitch based on one of the company's biggest clients so that I could use it as a kind of audition piece. He said it would show initiative – and he'd make sure the company's creative directors looked at it when it was ready.'

Rowan paused and Peter shifted uncomfortably. His fists were already balled in his lap. He wasn't *quite* sure where this was going, but it wasn't going to be good, was it?!

'Anyway, I did it – I threw myself into it and then handed it over to Ben.'

'And he didn't show them?' said Peter in disgust.

'Oh, he did!' said Rowan with a scowl. 'And passed the entire thing off as his own work.'

'So you kneed him in the balls?' said Peter.

'After a two-month delay,' said Rowan. 'That happened when my work won him an award which was announced at the teambuilding event. I just lost it. We'd already split up by then of course…'

'And they suspended you?' said Peter, appalled.

'They didn't believe a word I said,' said Rowan. 'We'd done such a good job of keeping our relationship quiet, and when I accused him of stealing my work, it was like… I don't know… in their eyes, I just turned into this deranged stalker.'

'But there's no way they can suspend you for that?'

'Seems a physical attack on your boss is more than just frowned at, no matter how well-earned it was,' said Rowan. 'According to HR, I'm just lucky Ben didn't want to press charges!'

'It's so unfair though!' said Peter.

'Yeah, well…'

'When will they take you back?' said Peter.

'Supposedly, there's an ongoing investigation,' she said. 'So… maybe when that's finished? But, as far as they're concerned, I'm a liability with a screw loose. Honestly, I think they're just jumping through the necessary hoops that will let them sack me.'

'Bloody hell!' said Peter. 'And no one here knows why you're back?'

'Connor knows… and Ivy of course. I just didn't want everyone else to know. Like I said – they'd be on the next flight to Edinburgh to try and sort it out for me,' she said with a fond smile.

'I can just imagine Olive with a pitchfork!' said Peter mildly. 'Frankly – I'd be tempted to join her. Seriously though, I'm really sorry for what happened.'

Rowan shrugged. 'Serves me right for thinking I could try for something a bit different with my life.'

'No - that's not right!' said Peter quickly, horrified that Rowan's one shot of trying to do something with her amazing talent had ended in such a hideous mess. 'It wasn't your fault that idiot stole your work. I mean… that's theft! He should be the one under investigation. Frankly – he deserved those crushed gooseberries!'

'HR don't agree, I'm afraid,' said Rowan. 'Anyway – now you know I'm not some kind of international spy in hiding, do you mind if we enjoy the rest of our evening? I don't really want to think about that mess anymore - I've already wasted enough time worrying about it.'

'You've got it!' said Peter with a decided nod.

Ten minutes later, Rowan pulled the car onto a grassy spot, killed the engine and hopped out. Grabbing their bag of ice cream, Peter followed suit, staring across the causeway at the cottage on The Dot.

'Are we walking over?' said Peter, spotting a little boat bobbing next to the shore below them.

'The water's low enough that we could use the causeway, but I thought we'd take the boat anyway,' said Rowan. 'You don't mind, do you? Only, we've got so much shopping to take across, plus the last thing I want is for the pair of us to get stranded on the other side when the tide comes back up again.'

'I'd love to go in the boat,' said Peter, doing his best not to let his excited inner six-year-old show too much. 'Erm... so how often does your brother manage to get stranded on one side while the boat's stuck on the other shore?'

'Yeah... pretty often! Rowan laughed. 'At least to begin with until he got the hang of things. He's definitely had to call Mr Harris a few times and beg him to bring the boat over so that he could get to work on time. Sometimes he ends up sleeping at the Tallyaff when he gets stranded on this side!'

'It really is like another world up here,' said Peter, staring around.

'You'd better believe it!' said Rowan. 'Come on... let's grab the shopping.'

CHAPTER 20

ROWAN

Rowan couldn't believe she'd just told Peter everything. It was so embarrassing... but in a way, she felt so much lighter.

When she'd told Connor about it, he'd been sympathetic, but then - in his usual way - he'd made a joke about Edinburgh being littered with her exes. He definitely hadn't quite grasped the fact that the main source of hurt had come from the fact that Ben had stolen her work and passed it off as his own. It was the first time she'd allowed herself anywhere near doing something creative since she'd left Crumcarey – and it had backfired spectacularly.

Peter had understood though - even if he *had* winced and crossed his legs when she'd told him about what she'd done!

She shot a quick look over her shoulder towards the back of the boat, where Peter was perched amongst their bags of shopping. He was staring across the water with a huge, goofy smile on his face. He had his ever-present notebook perched precariously on his lap, and if Rowan didn't know any better, she'd guess that he was quickly falling under Crumcarey's spell.

It only took a few minutes for them to reach The Dot, and Rowan quickly tied the boat up before helping Peter to unload their shopping.

'Hey,' said Peter, the minute he stepped through the front door of Connor's cottage. 'Why does this place feel so familiar?'

Rowan watched in amusement as he wandered through to the kitchen, staring around and taking in every detail as he went.

'Seriously,' he said, 'why do I feel like I've been here before?'

'Well,' said Rowan, 'Connor did all the work on this place… and he did most of the work on Groatie Buckie Cottage too – maybe that's why?'

Peter peered around him again, then nodded slowly. 'It's all the woodwork. It's got a certain style to it.'

Rowan nodded.

'Blimey – talk about a talented family!' said Peter. 'So Connor works as a carpenter as well as captaining the ferry?'

'Nah!' laughed Rowan. 'He just did this up for himself.'

'And Groatie Buckie Cottage?'

'He was just making himself useful!' said Rowan,

shoving the ice cream into the freezer and turning to start unpacking their bags.

'Blimey – he'd make a fortune on the mainland!' said Peter, still staring around with wide eyes. 'It's gorgeous in here.'

'Ha! Connor move away from Crumcarey? Not in a million years!'

Rowan quickly shut her mouth. Talk about blundering straight into the perfect opportunity for Peter to ask why she was the polar opposite of her big brother!

'Shall we go and look for your paintings, then?' said Peter.

Rowan turned to him with a smile, grateful for the deft change of subject – whether he'd done it on purpose or not.

'Do you mind if we eat first?' she said. 'I'm ravenous. I always get this way when I stay here – I think it's the sea air!'

'Good call,' said Peter with a nod. 'You get the kettle on for the pasta and I'll make a start on the sauce.'

As the pair of them moved around the little kitchen in companionable silence, Rowan couldn't resist stealing sneaky looks at this stranger who already felt oddly familiar... and it wasn't just because she'd had the unexpected delight of catching a glimpse of him without a stitch on! It was like she'd known him for years. She felt completely comfortable with Peter – which was weird considering he already knew one of her most closely-guarded secrets… and had come very close to unearthing the other one too.

Rowan wouldn't be volunteering that information any time soon, though. She'd never told anyone why she'd stopped painting so suddenly. Even though Olive could probably hazard a fair guess and Connor almost definitely knew, she'd never actually said the words out loud.

'Earth to Rowan?'

'Sorry!' she laughed, feeling her cheeks heat up as she stared at him, slightly dazed by his tanned, bare forearms. He'd rolled up his shirtsleeves and clearly meant business. 'I was away with the fairies!'

'I could see that,' said Peter. 'You definitely need some food! I was just wondering where your brother keeps the salt?'

Rowan grinned and moved to stand next to him. How long had she been daydreaming for?! His chopping board was already piled high with finely chopped onions and red peppers.

'Here,' she said, leaning across him to reach for the cupboard above his head. She grabbed the little ceramic bowl of sea salt, willing her hand not to shake. She could feel the warmth of him through her jumper.

'Here,' she said again, her voice tiny as she fought a weird tingle as it whispered across her skin.

'Ta,' said Peter, taking the bowl from her without taking his eyes off her face.

Rowan paused, far too aware of her breath and his

warmth and the fact that she could so easily lean in and kiss him right now.

Ah, crap. This wasn't meant to happen. She'd only set eyes on him for the first time yesterday!

'Sorry,' said Peter, taking a step back to give her some space.

She knew he was being polite, but Rowan couldn't help feeling a tiny bit disappointed. For one brief second there she'd thought... hoped... that he might be thinking about kissing her too.

Rowan gave herself a little shake and went to pour the boiling water over the pasta shells.

Damnit!

Her lips were still tingling in anticipation. Hell, she didn't even know if the man was single!

'So,' she said, casually trying to break the awkward silence. 'Erm... so... how does your other half cope with you gallivanting all over the world for a living?'

Smooth, Rowan! Very casual!

'Oh – she copes brilliantly,' Peter laughed. 'Can you put the heat under the frying pan?'

Rowan nodded, turning to the hob as she felt something inside her curl up in disappointment.

'Considering she doesn't exist, she really doesn't mind how much gallivanting I do!' continued Peter, blithely unaware of the weird impact his throwaway joke had just had on her.

'Well,' she said quickly, 'that's good. I mean... not

that you're single, but that there isn't a heartbroken woman back at home!'

'No heartbreaks in my past,' said Peter with a shrug. 'I've never been with anyone long enough for that kind of upset!'

'Really?' said Rowan in surprise, then clapped her hand over her mouth. 'Sorry, that sounded really mean. I just meant... how?!' She gestured awkwardly at him, making him laugh again.

'I just love to travel too much. I've met some amazing people, and don't get me wrong... I'm not a monk!'

Rowan screwed up her nose.

'Sorry,' he said quickly, 'TMI! What I mean is – I love my work-'

'Even when you're sent to a damp Scottish island instead of the tropics?' she said.

'Even then,' he grinned. 'Still, it's not exactly conducive to a long-term relationship, is it?.'

'I guess not,' said Rowan with an awkward shrug.

'And you?' he said. 'I mean... how recently did you and Ben... you know?'

'Blow up?' she said, stirring the pasta a little more vigorously than was strictly necessary.

'Yeah,' said Peter, sounding apologetic.

'About six months ago,' she sighed.

'So you're still getting over him?' said Peter.

'Actually, no,' said Rowan, surprised that it was true. 'I think I was over him before we even split up! Then he pulled that stunt with my work... I mean, I'm not going to waste my energy being hung up on someone like that!'

'Okay – I have to say, I love your attitude!' said Peter, looking impressed.

'Life's too short to waste it like that. I totally understand grieving lost love... but I never loved him... so...'

Peter nodded. 'Here, let's get these in the pan!' he said, passing her the board of finely chopped veggies.

Rowan took it from him and carefully scraped the multi-coloured mess into the pan, setting it sizzling.

∽

Just twenty minutes later, they were already halfway through two heaped bowls of pasta covered in the most delicious sauce Rowan had ever tasted.

Peter had been entertaining her with tales from his travels around the world, and with the pressure of having to talk about her own mess of a life lifted, Rowan was really starting to enjoy herself.

Not only could the man cook like an angel, but Peter also had a lovely, self-deprecating sense of humour. He'd had her in stitches as he'd told her about getting stranded in Antigua when his editor had accidentally sent all his return travel documents to another writer – who just happened to be in Norway at the time.

'I can think of worse places to get stuck!' said

Rowan. 'I'm jealous of how many places you've seen. I've always wanted to travel more.'

'Where would you go if you could go anywhere?' said Peter.

Rowan took a long sip of her bubbly pink squash, thinking hard. 'There are so many places I'd love to see… but I think… Alaska first?'

'I wasn't expecting that!' said Peter.

'There's this beach where glass buoys get washed up, and you can get a pilot to fly you out there… it's so remote! I'd love to see that,' she sighed.

'It sounds amazing,' said Peter, mopping up the last of his sauce with a chunk of bread. 'I'd love to see that too – hey, let's go together!'

Rowan grinned at him. She knew he was messing around, but she couldn't help the warm glow that had just kindled in her stomach at the thought. Just the idea of seeing such a beautiful place with Peter for company sounded like a dream.

'Hey!' she said. 'When we're done here, rather than driving you straight back to the cottage, how about I take you over to the cliffs to see the puffins?'

'Really?' said Peter, his eyes lighting up. 'I'd love to!'

'Brilliant,' said Rowan as a ripple of excitement went through her. Why did it feel like he'd just agreed to a first date?

No, Rowan – this is just work for him!

'Cool,' said Rowan, trying to keep her voice calm and casual.

'In that case... we'd better get hunting for those paintings, hadn't we?' said Peter.

Damn. She'd been having such a lovely time, she'd forgotten why they were here in the first place.

'Yeah,' said Rowan. 'Okay – let's get this over with!'

'You know... if you really don't want me to use your work in the book, you can just tell me,' he said, watching her intently. 'It's not a problem - I could still do the photos instead'

'Thanks,' said Rowan. She was so grateful to him for giving her an easy way out of the whole thing... but she couldn't help but notice the little bubble of disappointment that seemed to form in her chest as he said it.

That was new! Maybe this was something she needed to do after all. For Crumcarey, if not for herself. Besides, for some inexplicable reason, she trusted Peter to do what was best for the book and for Crumcarey. It was obvious after listening to his stories that he really cared about his work.

'No,' she said after a long pause, 'let's do it. If Connor has managed to stash anything away that you'd like to use, then I'm okay with it.'

'Okay!' said Peter. 'Let's start searching.'

CHAPTER 21

PETER

*P*eter didn't know what he'd been expecting... maybe a magical mystery tour through the cottage while they searched every single cupboard for a portfolio of precious paintings. In the end, it took Rowan less than five minutes to locate Connor's hiding place.

'My brother's not exactly a man of mystery!' said Rowan as she flipped open the wooden trunk at the bottom of his and Ivy's double bed, revealing what looked like a nest of totally random junk. 'He always used to stash his most precious things under his bed. I guess this trunk is the adult version of that!'

'Nice upgrade,' laughed Peter.

'Bingo – here we go!' said Rowan as she moved an ancient stuffed donkey and a tin box gently out of the way, and then lifted out an old, flattened cardboard box. It had been tied up with several lengths of string.

While Rowan sat on the bed and worked at the knots, Peter found himself unable to look away from the trunk. It looked like Connor had carefully preserved the most precious parts of his childhood – an old sticker book, a stack of ancient comics, a signed cricket bat and -weirdest of all – half a skateboard.

'What happened to this?' he said, leaning down and spinning one of the wheels lightly with his finger.

'God – don't ask!' laughed Rowan, craning her neck to take a look. 'He begged and begged our parents for one, then the first day he got it, he rolled it right off a cliff up at Craigie Head!'

'With him still on it?!' said Peter.

'Thankfully not!' laughed Rowan. 'He kind of did this sideways dive onto the path, but the board carried on!'

'Jeez!' breathed Peter. 'Bet your parents were glad he was okay!'

'It was the only time I ever heard dad lose it – I mean properly lose it!' said Rowan. 'Mum was all white and shaky, but Dad just went ballistic! The fear, I guess...'

Rowan turned back to the knots, and Peter gave his head a little shake, trying to rid himself of the image of a young boy heading towards the edge of a cliff at lightning speed.

'So... how come he's still got the board?' said Peter.

'That half washed up a week later about two miles south,' said Rowan. 'The other half never turned up.'

'Poor Connor!' said Peter.

'Nah – it gave him bragging rights for weeks!' said Rowan. 'There!' she added triumphantly as the mess of string fell away from the cardboard.

'Excellent!' said Peter, moving to sit on the opposite side of the bed to her. He looked at Rowan, expecting her to flip the cardboard open. He couldn't wait to see what else he had to work with!

Rowan, however, had one hand firmly on the cover of the makeshift folder, and she was biting her lip.

'You okay?' he asked.

She nodded, then shook her head.

'Look,' she said, 'I've got no idea what Connor's got in here. I know it's what we've been looking for because this is how I always used to bundle my work up… but… well, they might be total crap, okay?'

'It's fine,' said Peter with a nod. 'It's simple - if they're crap, we don't use them. And remember, you get the final say over what I can and can't use.'

'Really?' said Rowan, eyeballing him warily.

'I promise we won't include anything you don't want to,' he said. 'Though I reserve the right to argue the point if you're just being stubborn,' he added with a wink.

Rowan smiled at that. 'You just sounded weirdly like my big brother!'

'Sounds like a good guy,' laughed Peter, relieved to see the fear leave her face again.

'He has his moments,' said Rowan. 'Right, let's see what rubbish the sentimental git kept, shall we?'

Peter leaned in as Rowan shifted the portfolio between them and flipped it open. As expected, the very first image took his breath away. Wide, moody skies above sweeping coral sands, and a tiny lighthouse on a distant point, glowing in a light that was almost supernatural.

He took a deep breath. He already understood enough about Rowan to know that gushing about her work would probably result in her clamming up again, so he took a beat before saying anything.

'Where abouts is this?' he said.

'The far end of Big Sandy, looking north,' said Rowan.

Peter chanced a quick look at her face. She was looking at the painting and it was obvious from her expression that she was taking in the colour and lines with nothing but a critical eye.

Peter took it gently out of her hands and laid it aside. He didn't say it out loud, but this was the start of his "definitely include at all costs" pile.

Next in line was a trio of perfect puffins on a cliff edge, then a swallow swooping over an abandoned stone building.

'My bird phase,' laughed Rowan, shifting them aside before Peter could get at them.

'Actually – I think a birdlife section's a great idea!' said Peter.

'Bit specialist?' said Rowan, screwing up her nose.

'Yes – but that's a huge market – and a good one for Crumcarey to tap into. Birders are just the kind of visitors you want to attract. They don't give two hoots about the weather – they just want a glimpse of the island's unusual birdlife!'

'Well, there's plenty of that,' said Rowan with a shrug.

Peter could feel a bubble of excitement rising in his chest. These paintings were throwing up so many new possibilities... and they'd only just started.

Rowan flipped through a few more paintings at speed, listing off their locations as she went.

'Craigie Head. Craigie Head again. I wasn't meant to go up there on my own, so naturally, it became my favourite place in the world!' she laughed. 'Big Sandy. Not Sandy.'

'A cowrie!' said Peter as she uncovered a study that was different to the sweeping landscapes. An extreme close-up showing the curves, ridges and blush pink tinge of the little shell.

'That's right - a Groatie Buckie!' said Rowan.

'I love it!' said Peter.

Oops... there he went with the gushing. He glanced at Rowan, but she was smiling at him.

'There should definitely be a section for Groatie Buckies!' she said. 'I'll show you some of the best places to find them. They're tricky to see to start with – but there are all sorts of myths and legends about them you can research. They're meant to be lucky.'

'Can we go on a hunt tomorrow?' said Peter. He couldn't help it – his inner child was starting to shine through again.

Rowan grinned across at him, and he felt something melt inside him. This wasn't just his usual level of excitement at discovering a new place – it was the thought of doing it with Rowan at his side that was making him feel practically giddy.

'Okay,' said Rowan, her voice gentle as she smiled at him warmly. 'We can go hunting tomorrow.' She reached across the bed and covered his hand with hers.

Peter froze, staring at her. There was no way – absolutely no way – he'd ever make a first move after hearing what she'd been through… but that didn't mean he didn't want to. If she leaned across and kissed him right now, he definitely wasn't going to complain. It had practically been torture not to reach for her while they'd been cooking together… and eating with her foot occasionally brushing his under the table had been about as distracting as it got.

But still… he didn't move.

Rowan seemed to be drifting closer to him, and Peter felt his heart thudding in his chest. Surely, she could hear it? He felt like he was about to drown in the sound… but then her hand was gone, and she was staring back down at her paintings as though the moment had never even happened.

Peter blinked stupidly, feeling like he was surfacing from the depths of a dream, waking up just as it was about to get to the good bit.

'Did you spot the other box Connor's got in that trunk?' said Peter, standing up and doing his best to shake out the feeling that something had just shifted between the pair of them.

Rowan looked up at him enquiringly and shook her head.

He moved to the trunk and gently lifted out a shoebox that was missing a part of its lid. He'd glimpsed something that looked suspiciously like a bunch of old paintbrushes through the tear.

Sure enough, there were at least a dozen of them, held together with an ancient rubber band. There was also a scruffy wooden box that he would bet anything held a set of watercolours, a ceramic palette and even a little saucer that still held the tell-tale stains of dried-out paint around its lip.

'Wow!' said Rowan. 'This stuff used to come everywhere with me.' She paused, and Peter watched as her face became thoughtful again. 'I can't believe he kept it all this time.'

'I can't believe you stopped painting,' said Peter, setting the box on the bed and starting to flick through the still-unsorted pile of paintings.

'Yeah, well... life changes, people move on,' she sighed.

'Wow!' said Peter, coming to rest on a piece that

quite literally took his breath away. 'This one's beautiful.'

Rowan craned her neck to look but didn't say anything.

'It's definitely going in the book,' he said, angling it so that he could get a better look in the lamplight. It was an old church – or kirk, as they were called up here. The old stonework of the building was wreathed by a bank of storm clouds, the blues deepening to an almost purple as they threatened rain. But a ray of sunlight pierced the clouds and touched a green mound sitting between the graves.

'No,' said Rowan, her voice flat. 'Not that one.'

'No… you're right,' said Peter, 'it's got water damage! Look – it's like it got dripped on… I'm guessing those storm clouds reached you sooner than you were expecting!'

Rowan shook her head but didn't say anything.

'Such a shame…' said Peter. 'I think it's my favourite so far.'

He paused, staring at it. He had to have this painting in the book! People adored the old churches and always loved the sections that included myths, legends and snippets of history surrounding them.

'Maybe you could re-do this one for the book?' he said. 'Connor's kept your paints… it's perfect!'

'No,' said Rowan.

'But…'

'No, Peter,' she said again.

Before he knew what was happening, she'd grabbed the paper from his hands. Then with quick, sharp movements, she tore the painting in half, and then in half again before stuffing the fragments into her jeans pocket.

'Rowan!' he gasped. 'Oh my god – what did you just do?!'

'I've got no idea why Connor had that – I binned it years ago,' she said, her voice heavy.

'But-'

'I think it's time to take you back to the cottage,' she said, gathering the rest of the paintings together in a heap and wrapping the cardboard roughly around them.

'But... did you still want to go and see the puffins?' he said. What the hell had just happened? Her face had become wooden – pale and almost lifeless.

'Not tonight. I'm sorry Peter.' Rowan shook her head.

'Okay,' he said, frowning. He had no idea what was going on, but there was no point pushing her, was there? She might take it out on the rest of the paintings otherwise! 'We can do it another time.'

Rowan nodded, not saying anything.

'Are you sure you're okay to drive me back?' he said. She nodded again.

'And... do you mind if I take the rest of the paintings to look through? Just so I know what we've got to work with and make a bit of a plan?'

Rowan froze, her hand resting on the cardboard folder and for one horrible moment, Peter thought she was going to back out of the whole thing. Then, with a deep breath, she handed the bundle over to him without a word.

'Thanks,' he said, tucking them protectively against his chest before hurrying to follow her stiff, silent figure downstairs.

∼

Peter shut the door of Groatie Buckie Cottage quietly behind him and stared around the kitchen. After a couple of seconds of not knowing what on earth to do with himself, he strode forwards and placed the cardboard portfolio of precious paintings carefully onto the kitchen table.

Feeling like he needed something to take the edge off what had just happened, he grabbed a bottle of wine from the stash that Olive had sent him. He poured a generous glass over near the sink, not wanting to risk even the slightest splash or spill anywhere near Rowan's work. Somehow though, he had a feeling she'd be relieved to have an excuse to toss the rest of the paintings in the bin along with the one she'd torn to shreds in front of his eyes.

'What a waste!' he sighed, taking a sip of his drink.

He still had no idea what that had been about, but he had a sneaking suspicion there was far more to it than Rowan wanting to bin the painting just because of a bit of water damage. That painting had clearly triggered something. Why else would she have practically booted him out of Connor's cottage?

The journey back here had been the weirdest twenty minutes of his life. A completely silent boat ride, followed by a trip in the car where Rowan had probably managed to force out a maximum of five words. He simply couldn't understand how they'd gone from her almost kissing him, to him standing here alone in the silent kitchen.

Ah well! He was here to do a job, not get dragged into someone else's problems…

The thing was, after Rowan's strange behaviour he was pretty sure that it would be a far safer bet to message Mel and tell her to forget all about the local artist he'd discovered.

Peter knew in his heart of hearts that Rowan was a flight risk – she could just decide that she didn't want to let him use her work at any moment, and that would be that. Working with her would put his professional life at risk… not to mention his personal life. Because there was no doubt about it, Peter could feel how attached he was getting to this funny, sassy, broken, secretive, beautiful woman.

'Hell!' he muttered, staring at the cardboard folder again. He knew what he *should* do… but right now, it wasn't what he *wanted* to do.

Clearing the table, he quickly wiped it down and

made sure there weren't any splashes or crumbs anywhere to be seen. Then, with a deep breath, he opened the folder and started to work through the paintings.

The minute he reached the bottom of the pile, he did the same thing in reverse, but this time, he dug his mobile phone out and photographed each one as he went. They weren't the best photographs in the world, but they'd do the job.

He quickly grabbed his coat and let himself back out of the cottage, mobile phone firmly in hand, his eyes on the screen as he went. There had to be some signal around here somewhere!

Peter knew this was a risk. He'd told Rowan they would get Olive to send the photos through to Mel in the morning… but suddenly, he wasn't willing to wait until then. What if Rowan changed her mind about the whole thing and stopped him from sending them? No – this was one of those occasions where he'd much rather beg forgiveness than ask permission.

'Come on, come on,' he muttered, waving his phone around. Nothing.

He stomped down onto the beach, slipping and sliding, the pebbles shifting under his weight as he made his way to the water's edge.

'There!' he said, as a tiny hint of signal popped up on the screen before disappearing again. He was poised to send the blasted email the minute he found it again.

He held his mobile high… nothing. He took another step… then another…

'Bingo!' he said with triumph. He quickly hit send, muttering a little prayer as he waited.

Message Sent!

'Yes!' he cheered, then let out a yelp of surprise as a wave lapped right up over his feet, soaking through his trainers and into his socks.

Great!

He stared down with a sigh.

Wait, what was that?!

Peter bent down, ignoring his soggy feet, and carefully picked up a tiny, blush-pink shell. Domed, with little ridges and an unmistakable opening on one side. A Groatie Buckie.

CHAPTER 22

ROWAN

Rowan sighed and kicked at the bedclothes. She'd been tossing and turning all night and now she was hot and bothered. Even the simple touch of the rucked-up cotton cover was annoying her. The usually cosy goose-down duvet suddenly felt like a straitjacket.

She heaved herself up into a half-sitting position and peered towards the curtains. Daylight was making its way in around the edges, but frankly, that didn't mean much on Crumcarey at this time of year. They were so far north that it just stopped bothering to get fully dark. The night sky just faded to a light dusk and then the sun changed its mind and reappeared like a belligerent toddler refusing to be put down for its nap.

Rowan had no idea what the time was. She'd left her phone downstairs the previous night - not wanting to risk sending a message to her brother, griping about the painting. She hadn't wanted to be tempted into contacting Peter either, come to that... a long grovelling apology by text probably wouldn't quite have the right ring to it – especially if it ended with her pleading with him for a snog!

They'd come so close!

Rowan shivered. She couldn't think about that right now!

She flopped back onto the pillows and thumped the duvet as it followed her, promptly trying to smother her again. Right... she had two choices. She could either turn over, bury her head in her arms and do her best to get some sleep... or she could get up and go downstairs.

Whatever the time was, she couldn't bear the idea of lying here any longer, listening to the quiet, settling sounds of the old cottage and the sea outside the window. It should be lovely and restful, but all she could think about was the way she'd behaved towards Peter the previous evening. The poor bloke had no idea why that painting had hit a nerve... but seeing that bloody thing had been a strange kind of tipping point, and she'd gone right over the edge.

It didn't help that she was absolutely certain she'd thrown it into the rubbish bin years ago. Connor must have decided to save it when she'd had her back turned. She'd actually quite enjoyed seeing the other pieces... but not that one. It had been the final painting she'd ever completed - the last thing she'd done before she'd packed up her paint and pallets for the very last time.

Rowan kicked her legs out of the bed, wincing slightly as her head pounded at the sudden movement. Yuck! If that wasn't enough of a clue, the sour aftertaste in her mouth reminded her that she'd launched a full-frontal attack on one of Connor's bottles of wine last night in an attempt to drown the painful memories.

Reaching for the glass of water on her bedside table, Rowan took a long sip. She was going to be like the walking dead today. Ah well – there was no point staying in bed any longer. She'd go down to the kitchen, check her phone, grab a hot drink and maybe try to have a snooze on the sofa if there was time before she was due to meet Peter at the Tallyaff.

The thought of seeing him again made her squirm slightly. She had so much apologising to do! Especially as they'd almost...

It was almost a kiss. I know it was!

Knowing that made everything worse. She'd so wanted to lean into him, to kiss him and see where the moment took them. Instead, that painting had taken her straight back to one of the worst days of her life and ruined everything.

Rowan jumped to her feet. She couldn't think about that again right now otherwise she was going to drive herself mad! Shoving on a pair of slouchy jogging bottoms, a thick pair of woolly socks and a motheaten cardigan, she headed downstairs.

The minute she got to the kitchen, Rowan regretted her decision to get out of bed – and not just because the clock was declaring that it was exactly five-thirty – a particularly unhelpful time of day. It was too late to get any decent sleep, but too early to head out and do anything useful.

'Balls,' she breathed, looking at the kitchen table.

There in front of her was the real reason she wished she was back in bed with the duvet firmly over her head. She'd forgotten that the kitchen had seen an awful lot of frantic action last night – on top of the ridiculous amount of wine and sobbing.

Rowan rubbed her face roughly and stared at the mess on the table, her eyes going straight to the torn strips of painting that were now held together with a haphazard arrangement of sticky tape and red-wine splotches. She leaned on the back of a chair to steady herself, unable to take her eyes off the marks on the painting that Peter had taken for raindrops.

No Peter, they're teardrops.

The torn shoebox was there too, its contents spread all over the table. Her old, beloved paintbox was wide open, and her ceramic pallet was splattered with colour.

She'd... painted?

Yes, there was a second wine glass on the table, filled with muddy water where she'd used it to wash her brushes... so where were the...

'Bloody hell!' she laughed, shaking her head.

She'd just spotted a wodge of paper that had been half-hidden by the shoebox. The top sheet looked like a rainbow had been murdered on it. Reaching out, she picked up the pile and did her best to separate the wavy, oversaturated pages. The twenty or so sheets of expensive watercolour paper were splattered with a kaleidoscope of colours. A total mess... a moment of unblocking and pure insanity ignited by grief and red wine.

There was something about the sight of the carnage that made her feel better... though she didn't have the faintest clue why. Ah well, maybe she'd be able to work it out as she cleared up the chaos!

Rowan grabbed the shoddily mended painting from the table. It was going back where it belonged – along with the rest of this drunken escapade! She strode across the kitchen, hit the pedal of the bin and dumped last night's daubings straight inside. Then she went to do the same with the torn and mended painting... but hesitated. Before she even knew what she was doing or why, she folded it up again and thrust it into her back pocket.

'Tea!' she gasped.

～

Rowan approached the old stone walls slowly. She had her hands buried deep inside her fleece pockets as she stared fixedly at the ancient walls of Crumcarey's kirk.

This had once been one of her favourite places. The island's graveyard always used to have the ability to soothe her – but now...

She felt her steps falter the nearer she got to the old wooden gates, until she ground to a halt in front of them.

So... she still couldn't face it? Even after all these years?

Rowan swallowed hard. She reached out to lift the latch on the gate but drew back again as though she'd been stung. She stared desperately into the graveyard for a moment... and then sagged.

Not this morning.

Perhaps not ever.

Rowan sighed, closing her eyes for a moment. She was so tired. Her strong cup of tea had breathed unexpected life into her weary body, so she'd dumped her plan to grab a snooze on the sofa in favour of getting outside and enjoying Crumcarey in the early morning light.

She'd briefly entertained the idea of heading up to Craigie Head to visit the puffins, but thoughts of Peter had changed her mind. It wouldn't be fair to go and see them without him – not after last night.

So instead, she'd decided to come here. But now, that initial shot of caffeine had worn off - and she wasn't quite sure what she'd been thinking. Rowan had had some kind of vague hope that getting her paints and brushes out again last night might mean that she'd managed to release this block too… that after all these years, she'd be able to visit them.

Forcing herself to open her eyes, she drew the damaged painting out of her back pocket and opened it up. She rested it against the old stone wall and did her best to smooth out the creases.

The scene she'd painted was around the back of the kirk, tucked away and just out of view from her vantage point by the gate. Rowan had always been grateful that it wasn't visible from the road… until now. If only she could see them from here without having to go in!

Thankfully, all her tears seemed to have fallen the previous night. Rowan blinked her tired, dry eyes, trying to ignore the fact that her heart felt like it was calling out – yearning to speak to the two stones just out of sight.

No. Not the stones…

Quickly folding the painting back up, she tucked it back into her pocket and turned away from the kirk. This had been a terrible idea. She needed to get away from the graveyard. She'd would go for a walk on the beach instead and do her best to clear her head before she had to meet Peter. Rowan wanted to apologise properly – and the last thing she wanted was for him to have to deal with another emotional outburst.

Yes, a blast of sea air and a mooch along the sand was exactly what she needed right now.

~

Rowan knew she was going to be ridiculously early. She wasn't due to meet Peter until nine, but the wind had decided to start whipping the waves into an early-morning frenzy, and she'd had to abandon her beach walk. She'd stuck it out for as long as she could – but her extremities were starting to seize up from the constant buffeting. It might be summer, but that didn't mean it was a good idea to leave your bobble hat at home!

'Rookie mistake!' she muttered, doing her best to drag her fingers through her hair and wincing as she encountered a veritable bird's nest of knots.

Rowan half-wondered whether she should nip back to the cottage on The Dot before meeting Peter. It was going to be bad enough trying to explain her behaviour, adding *scarecrow-dragged-backwards-through-a-hedge* vibes into the mix wasn't exactly going to help her feel calm and confident, was it?

Glancing at the clock on the dashboard, she hesitated. She'd have plenty of time to get to the cottage... but she was only five minutes away from the Tallyaff, and Olive would be cooking breakfast. Maybe she could scrounge a nice big fry-up and beg the use of one of the bathrooms to make herself look a bit more presentable instead.

Rowan's stomach gave a loud growl. Well... there was her answer! Besides, if she was being honest, she wasn't entirely sure that she'd manage to raise the bravery to leave the safety of the cottage for a second time.

Five minutes later, Rowan trundled to a halt in the guesthouse carpark and made sure that she had a white-knuckle grip on the door handle before she climbed out. She was just about to let herself into the cosy little porch when Olive flung the door open, making her jump.

'There you are!' she said, her face splitting into a beaming smile.

'Here I am?' said Rowan, her hand over her heart, reflexively giving her chest a little pat as though to reassure herself that everything was fine.

For a second, Olive's wide smile slipped, and she looked Rowan over from head to toe.

'Are you okay?'

'Bit windswept,' said Rowan with a smile, running her palm over her hair.

Olive shook her head. 'I didn't mean that! You're all white and... exhausted!'

Rowan kept the smile carefully on her face. She didn't want Olive to worry... nor did she want her to tell the rest of the island what was really wrong.

'I'm fine. Just a bit of a restless night, that's all!'

Olive frowned again. 'You know you can talk to me, don't you?' she said, her voice low and gentle now. 'Any time. Just me. I know what it's like on Crumcarey, but I'm here for you, okay?'

Rowan felt a lump of emotion lodge in her throat and she swallowed hard. She hadn't been fair to Olive, had she? She was a good friend, and she'd always been there for both her and Connor. Rowan had just never allowed her past a certain point... never turned to her or confided in her... maybe she'd been doing her old friend a disservice all these years. Perhaps she didn't need to keep everything so tightly locked inside anymore.

But not right now. This morning had already been hard enough, and the last thing Rowan wanted was to be an even bigger mess by the time Peter arrived.

'Thanks Olive,' she said, reaching out and giving her friend's arm a squeeze. 'You know - I'll take you up on that soon.'

'Good,' said Olive, smiling at her.

'Right now, though... I've got a favour to ask,' she said, trying to pull herself together. 'I need to borrow a hairbrush... and then I could do with some breakfast!'

'Perfect!' said Olive. 'You can join Peter. He'll be so chuffed you've finally arrived!'

'Finally?!' said Rowan. 'What time is it? I thought I was mega early!'

'You are... but he was earlier,' said Olive, her eyes sparkling. 'He's got news. Amazing news!'

'*What* news!' demanded Rowan, her heart threatening to beat its way out of her chest again.

This wasn't how this morning was meant to go!

'What news?!' she said again as Olive hadn't said

anything but was just standing there with a huge smile plastered on her face.

'I'm not going to spoil the surprise,' she said primly. 'Come on – come inside and I'm sure Peter will explain everything.'

CHAPTER 23

PETER

Considering he hadn't expected her to turn up at all, Peter was having a hard time staying in his seat as Rowan strolled into the Tallyaff with Olive bouncing along behind her.

He stared at Rowan, desperately trying to gauge how she'd taken the news... but it was practically impossible to read her. She looked tired, and a bit windswept... but the mad wind had breathed a beautiful pink flush into her cheeks, and her eyes looked all soft and sleepy.

Peter crossed his fingers underneath the table, willing himself to stay where he was rather than running to her and finishing what they'd almost started the day before.

He wanted to kiss her... then he wanted to find out what had been bugging her and help her solve it. Most of all - he wanted her to be excited about the news.

Right now, though, Rowan just looked curious... and maybe a little bit uneasy. The fingers of one hand were worrying at the nails of the other. She was nervous... but he wasn't sure what about.

'Hey,' she said, coming to a standstill a couple of feet from the table.

'You're here early!' said Peter, smiling at her.

'I was about to say the same thing,' she said.

She didn't return his smile, and Peter's heart dropped a little.

'Well... I fancied breakfast and I was feeling lazy. Want to join me?'

Rowan cocked her head. 'Sure you want me to interrupt your peaceful meal?'

'Are you kidding me?' he laughed. 'Please!'

'Okay,' she said with a little shrug, sinking into the chair opposite him.

Peter let out a tiny sigh of relief. 'So,' he said. 'What do you think?'

'About what?' she said.

'I haven't told her,' said Olive. 'Thought you'd like to do the honours!'

'Oh!' said Peter in surprise. He wasn't sure whether he should be pleased that he'd get to see Rowan's reaction for himself or gutted that it was now up to him to navigate telling her everything - and possibly face a re-run of yesterday in the process.

'What's going on?' said Rowan, her eyes flicking from him to Olive and then back again.

'First things first,' said Olive, 'what do you both want to eat – full fry-up?'

'Yes please!' said Peter. 'No Mushrooms for me though, ta!'

'I'll have his mushrooms,' said Rowan with a shadow of her usual grin. 'He can have my tomatoes if he wants them?'

'Deal!' said Peter.

'Won't be too long,' said Olive, bustling away.

'Peter,' said Rowan the minute Olive was out of earshot, 'I want to apologise for last night.'

Peter shook his head. He wanted to say there was no need, but before he'd even opened his mouth, she'd reached across the table and put her hand over his. There was something so desperate about the action... like she was lost and gripping onto his hand for support.

'I'm sorry,' she said. 'That painting I tore up...' she paused.

'You don't have to explain,' said Peter quietly.

'Why?' said Rowan with a frown. 'Did Olive already-?'

Peter shook his head quickly. 'No – of course not. I've not mentioned it to anyone... I just meant – it's obviously private... and really hard...'

'It is. But... I *want* to tell you... if that's okay?' she said, casting a nervy glance towards the bar, clearly checking that they were still alone.

'Of course it is,' said Peter.

'That painting was the last one I ever did,' said Rowan quickly. 'It was the last time I visited the graveyard... it was the day I said goodbye to both my parents.'

Peter watched her, barely daring to breathe. He didn't want to stop her from speaking now that she'd started. But... the pause was going on. She'd already stalled.

'Your parents?' he prompted gently, his heart squeezing at the lost look on her face.

'They died. On the same day.' She paused again. 'There was an accident on the mainland. Icy roads. They were both gone before the ambulance got to them.'

'I'm so sorry,' said Peter.

Rowan nodded silently and he felt her hand tighten over his.

'That painting... it was the only one I did after the accident. Of their graves. It was my way of saying goodbye.' She let out a long, shuddering breath. 'Those marks...'

'Weren't raindrops,' said Peter, his voice almost a whisper as the realisation dawned on him.

She shook her head. 'No.'

They'd been tears, hadn't they? And he'd gone and asked her to re-do the painting that must have taken a piece of her soul to complete.

'I'm so sorry,' he said. 'I would *never* have asked you to recreate it-'

'Don't apologise!' she said quickly. 'Please. How were you to know? I should have told you all this last night... but it was just such a shock to see it again. I binned that painting years ago. It was a constant reminder of everything I lost that day!' She paused again, and this time, she took her hand away from his to swipe at her eyes in irritation. 'Sorry,' she said with a watery smile.

'Don't be,' he said. 'I can't even begin to imagine... and then you had to deal with me bumbling around like an idiot.'

'It's always a bit difficult when I come back to Crumcarey,' she said with a long sigh. 'On one hand, I adore this place – it's home, you know? But on the other... they're not here anymore. And with all this talk of favourite places... and then giving you the paintings...'

'I've got them safe, don't worry,' he said quickly. 'I'll make sure you get them back before I leave.'

'It's not that,' said Rowan. 'It's just... it was always my parents who encouraged it, you know? My dad gave me those watercolours. I think they both saw it as a good way of keeping me out of trouble as a teen. They always loved seeing my work, and they'd make a big deal out of getting me to show it to them. After they'd gone... there was no one to show. God, that sounds ridiculous!' She let out a little laugh that sounded more like a sob.

'That's not ridiculous at all!' said Peter.

'Anyway... after that last one... I just stopped.'

'You've not painted since?' said Peter.

'Until last night,' she said quietly.

'That's... that's great!' said Peter in surprise.

'Nothing good, trust me,' she said. 'But in a way, it felt nice.'

She stopped and took in a long, deep breath. Peter watched as she seemed to shake herself out.

'Anyway – I'm sorry,' she said. 'I was a complete arse. You didn't deserve that.'

'You don't need to apologise,' said Peter. 'But... I think *I* do.'

Rowan cocked her head. 'What for?' she said, dabbing her eyes with the cuff of her jumper.

Peter had to resist the temptation to reach across the table and take her hand again... mainly so that she wouldn't do a runner when she heard what he had to say.

'Last night, I sent your paintings to Mel,' he said. 'I found a spot of signal down on the beach.'

'Oh!' said Rowan. 'Is that what's got Olive all worked up?'

Peter nodded, and even though he knew he was probably skating on seriously thin ice here, he couldn't help the smile spreading across his face.

'And?' said Rowan.

The single word made Peter smile even more broadly... because it was the enquiry of an artist awaiting feedback on her work.

'She adored them,' he said simply.

'She did?' said Rowan, blinking and clearly trying to take the words in.

'She did,' he confirmed. 'So much so that she wants to use them in the book.'

Rowan's eyes grew wide, and she sat completely still.

Oh hell...

'Does that mean-?'

'You get to decide,' said Peter quickly. 'It just means there will be a formal offer.'

'With the paintings I've already done?' said Rowan.

Peter nodded. 'Yes, but...'

'I knew there would be a but,' said Rowan.

'This is a good but,' he said. '*But* – if you are willing to paint more-'

'They're going to commission you to do the entire book!'

Olive's voice just behind him made Peter jump, and he turned to find her bouncing on the balls of her feet with excitement, the two large fry-ups she was carrying were threatening to spill right down the back of his neck.

'And-!' added Olive.

Then she caught Peter's eye.

'Sorry. You tell her!' she said, quickly moving to set the plates down on the table.

Peter turned back to Rowan with a rueful smile.

'Tell me what?!' said Rowan, sounding both amused and mildly desperate.

'Mel loved your work…' said Peter.

'Quite right too!' said Olive.

'And she's been up half the night,' said Peter.

'Hot flushes?' said Olive.

Peter snorted and Rowan clearly wanted to clap her hand over Olive's mouth to keep her quiet for a second.

'No… not flushes,' said Peter mildly. 'Rowan, she's been up badgering her team for most of the night.'

'Why?' said Rowan, looking even more confused.

'Well…' said Peter, trying to gauge how best to put this so he didn't scare her off.

'They want you and Peter to launch a whole series!' Olive blurted. 'Crumcarey will be the first and then…' she paused, noticing that Peter was glaring at her. 'Erm… I'll just be over here… enjoy your breakfast!'

She took two steps back and then started to wipe down the already gleaming table next to them.

'Shall we wait to talk it through?' Peter asked, his voice as low as possible, though Olive's frantic wiping had already slowed so that she could hear better.

Rowan shook her head. 'Just tell me!' she laughed.

'Mel loved your work. She forwarded it to the rest of the team last night, and then called them all, one by one to make sure they looked at it.'

'But… why the rush?' said Rowan. 'And what did Olive mean about the series?'

'Hurry up man!' said Olive, straightening up and turning back to him.

Peter ran a hand through his hair. This was *not* quite the sensitive approach he'd planned.

'They want you to help launch a new series. To come on board as the sole artist,' said Peter, wincing slightly as Rowan's eyes grew wide. 'They'd like to start with the Crumcarey guide – and then…'

'Then what?' said Rowan, clearly trying to digest it all. 'Then… travel? Or work from photos?'

'You'd be travelling,' said Peter steadily. 'Like I do.'

He didn't want to spook her any more than he already had.

'They're meeting right now to work out an offer!' said Olive. 'Congratulations Rowan!'

Rowan shook her head. 'I need…'

'To think about it?' said Peter, nodding.

Rowan shot him a grateful smile. 'Yep.'

'What's to think about?' demanded Olive.

Peter watched Rowan take a deep breath. Part of him wanted to step in, to protect her from the question, but he kept his mouth shut. This was her decision… how much she wanted to tell Olive and whether she wanted to take the job at all was up to her.

'I haven't done much painting since Mum and Dad died,' she said quietly.

Olive's hand went to her chest, and her face softened in instant sympathy.

'Not any, really,' Rowan added. 'It's been a long time... I'm not sure I can.'

'I'm sure it's not something you forget how to do, love,' said Olive gently.

Peter watched as Rowan smiled at the older woman, but he knew it wasn't her own skill she was debating… it was whether she would be able to overcome the emotional blocks that had been in place for so long. Whether she'd be able to work with the paints and brushes when they might unlock the deep well of sorrow she'd been avoiding for a very long time.

'Olive?' said Peter, 'do you reckon I could grab a coffee with this?' He nodded at his delicious-looking breakfast.

'Of course! One for you too, Rowan?'

Rowan nodded, though the question had clearly bounced straight off her. She was staring into the middle distance, looking dazed.

'Sorry,' whispered Peter. 'I really didn't want to do all this here, but Mel called me on the landline in Olive's office because she couldn't reach me on the mobile, and she didn't want to risk me not seeing her emails!'

Rowan gave him a half-smile. 'It's fine,' she said. 'Crumcarey has a way of drawing everything out of you in the end... and it's probably for the best. This place isn't made for secrets.'

'Yeah,' said Peter, glancing down at his rapidly cooling breakfast. He'd love nothing more than to tuck in, but until he knew she was okay, the idea of eating was ridiculous.

'Look,' said Rowan, visibly pulling herself together. 'I'm totally happy for you to use any of the existing paintings.'

'And what about some new ones?' he asked gently. 'And the job offer?'

'Can I think about it?' said Rowan. 'I mean, I'm not even sure if I *can* paint anymore.'

'Sure,' said Peter. He knew there was no point pushing her. He'd just have to protect her from Mel's excitement until she was ready.

'And... the job...' she said, chewing her lip. 'Who would I be working with? Would it be a mix of people or...'

'It would be me,' said Peter lightly. 'Mel wants me as the writer for the whole series.'

'Wow,' said Rowan. 'I mean, congratulations – that's incredible!'

'Thanks,' said Peter. He shot her a smile. It was what he'd wanted for so long. It was basically his dream assignment - no longer being sent off on a whim just because one of the other writers didn't fancy a trip.

'And... if I say no?' said Rowan slowly.

'Don't worry about that,' said Peter.

'I mean, it wouldn't ruin things for you?' said Rowan. 'They'd find another artist?'

Peter nodded. They might, but the reality was, this

entire project was very much inspired by Rowan's work.

'For what it's worth,' said Peter, 'I think we'd have a brilliant time. And I'd love to work with you.'

'Thanks,' said Rowan quietly.

'So... there's something else,' said Peter, wanting to break the tension.

Rowan looked at him, clearly unable to take much more before she'd had a cup of coffee.

'Don't look so worried,' laughed Peter. He shuffled in his seat and fumbled in his jeans pocket.

'Hold your hand out!' he said with a grin.

Rowan did so, looking confused.

Peter placed the tiny shell on her palm – blush pink with fine ridges and a tell-tale opening on one side.

'Your first Groatie Buckie!' Rowan cried, all the worry disappearing from her face in an instant. 'Yay! Where did you find it.'

'On the beach outside my cottage,' said Peter.

'Well, that's an extra good luck one then,' said Rowan with a soft smile.

He wanted to tell her that he'd found it right after he'd sent the email to Mel, but he bit his tongue. He wasn't going to do or say anything that might put extra pressure on her. This had to be Rowan's decision.

'Here,' she said, offering her hand so he could take the shell back.

'You keep it,' said Peter quietly. 'Extra good luck.'

CHAPTER 24

ROWAN

It had probably been one of the weirdest weeks of her life... and that was saying something.

Rowan and Peter had explored every inch of Crumcarey together, and she'd watched as he'd slowly but surely filled his ever-present notebook with all the island's hidden treasures. As for her, Rowan had made sure that she had her paints and sketchbook with her at all times.

At first, she'd felt incredibly awkward. It was one thing to be painting again after so many years, but it was an entirely different thing to be doing it when she had company!

Thankfully, her unease had lasted all of five seconds. The moment she'd settled on a picnic blanket on Big Sandy, picked up her brush and swirled it in the apricot-pink she'd mixed for the evening sky, all her fears had disappeared. As she laid down the first wash – the past and present came together on the page, and she'd released her sorrow into the painted sunset.

The pair of them quickly found an easy rhythm, working contentedly side-by-side, and Rowan soon found herself wondering what it would be like to take the experience beyond the shores of Crumcarey. She was all-in as far as the island's guidebook was concerned, but she still wasn't sure about the job offer.

Was she brave enough? And what about Peter – what did he think?

Ever since the news of Mel's offer – which was quickly followed by an email detailing an eyewatering salary - things between her and Peter had been strictly business. There hadn't been a repeat of that almost-kiss in Connor's bedroom, nor those delicious moments when their hands had touched.

All business.

Probably all for the best, too. After all, Peter would be leaving Crumcarey in just a few days, and even if Rowan *did* decide to take the job, they would be colleagues - and look at how well the last office romance had worked out for her!

Still, it didn't stop her from craving more. Rowan found herself desperately wishing that Peter might want it as much as she did.

There had been moments when she'd caught him watching her, and she'd briefly dared to hope that it might mean something... but he'd stayed silent. He was friendly and funny, but the closeness that had bloomed out of nowhere seemed to have vanished into thin air.

Rowan let out a long sigh as she pulled Connor's car up next to the sturdy wooden gates. Right now, she needed to put all that aside for an hour or two. She had a painting to do... the last one for the Crumcarey guidebook.

She stepped out of the car, grabbed her kit from the back and turned to stare across the old graveyard. It looked beautiful in the sunlight. The clouds had cleared, and though there was still quite a breeze blowing, it was a stunning evening. If only she could enjoy the setting for what it was... but Rowan was here to test her fears beyond anything else she'd faced since Peter had arrived on Crumcarey.

She rested her hand on the soft wooden curve of the gate, trying to find courage from somewhere to push her way through the barrier she hadn't crossed for more than a decade.

Closing her eyes and gripping her painting kit tightly with one hand, she pushed the gate with the other. Without opening her eyes, she stepped into Crumcarey's graveyard.

∽

It didn't take Rowan long to find her parents - but her face was already wet with tears by the time she dropped to her knees in front of the simple, twin stones that marked their final resting place.

Rowan might not have been here since her last goodbye, but Connor clearly had. Many of the graves around her were wild and overgrown with flowering weeds - making their own unkempt tributes to Crumcarey's lost souls. Not here though. The joint grave was neatly trimmed, and a lavender bush had been planted between the stones – her mother's favourite.

Rowan reached out and brushed the fragrant flowers as her tears water the little plant.

'Sorry I haven't visited,' she choked. 'It doesn't mean I don't miss you. Because I do – every day!'

She paused, her shoulders shaking as more than a decade's worth of swallowed sobs finally found their way out into the open. The wind swirled around her, sticking long strands of hair to her damp cheeks. Rowan brushed them away impatiently, taking deep, gulping breaths.

'I need your help,' she said when she'd calmed down enough to get the words out. 'I don't know what I should do. I'm scared that if I go with Peter… you'll think I've forgotten you. I'm scared that I could be happy… and you're not going to be here to see it. And I don't know what to do!'

Rowan stopped speaking as the tears took over, and she covered her face with her hands, letting the salty drops fall between her fingers. If only they were here with her right now. What would they say?

Why don't you get your paints out?

Rowan froze.

The words had just echoed in her head as clearly as anything. That had been her Mum's answer to everything.

Paint me a picture, Row.

And that was her dad.

Rowan dropped her hands and stared around, wide-eyed. She was alone in the sunlit churchyard, the only movement coming from the weeds as they were whipped around by the wind.

'Mum?' she whispered. 'Dad?'

The wind dropped to nothing and the whole world seemed to still around her.

Well… there was her answer.

Slowly, Rowan got to her feet and moved towards the old wooden bench near the wall. She took out her paper, her pallet and her brushes and started to paint.

∽

'If it isn't our local artist hard at work!'

The gentle greeting made Rowan look up in a daze – then she smiled. McGregor was sitting at her knee, and Mr Harris was making his way slowly between the stones towards her.

'Sorry to disturb,' he said, 'but I noticed the gate was open – and then I saw you and I wanted to say hello.'

'Hello,' said Rowan, smiling at him and patting the

bench for him to sit next to her. She reached out and ticked McGregor's ears. The dog blinked lazily and then flopped down across her feet. 'Anyway - you're not disturbing me – I've just finished,' she said, glancing down at the painting in her lap.

Mr Harris looked at her work and then nodded. 'I'm sure they're very proud,' he said quietly. 'I know I am. We all are.'

Rowan swallowed. 'Thanks,' she said, her voice slightly hoarse.

'Well, it's not every day one of our island daughters becomes a world-renowned artist, is it?' he said.

'I don't know about that!' laughed Rowan.

'Well... I hear you'll be off with your laddie all over the world soon,' he insisted. 'So it won't be long.'

'Two things... Peter's not *my* laddie,' said Rowan, 'and I've not decided whether to go yet.'

Mr Harris peered into her face for a moment. 'Yes you have,' he said with alarming certainty. 'And yes he is. Just because you've not got on with the job and done anything about it yet, that doesn't mean your souls haven't already sealed the deal.'

Rowan's mouth fell open and she stared at him.

'What?!' he demanded. 'Just saying!'

Rowan shut her mouth, not sure what to say. She had no idea what was going on right now, but something was definitely in the air.

'Anyway,' said the old farmer, 'that's a bonnie piece of work and no mistake.'

'Thanks,' said Rowan. 'I hope they like it.'

'For the book?' said Mr Harris.

Rowan paused for a moment and then nodded.

'They will,' he said. 'And your parents do too, by the way.'

She looked at him again.

'What?' said Mr Harris. 'They just told me.'

With that, he got to his feet, patted her gently on the shoulder and headed back around the corner towards the gate without another word, McGregor trailing behind him, wagging as he went.

Rowan shook her head, wondering if she'd just imagined the entire encounter. Then she shrugged. So what if she had!

Placing the new painting carefully onto the bench beside her, Rowan clambered to her feet and stretched. It was time to move on. Peter was waiting for her, and she needed to let him know that she'd just finished the last painting for the guidebook. Plus, she needed to give him her decision about the job… but first…

Rowan reached into her back pocket and carefully drew out the wad of paper she'd been carrying around with her all week. With gentle fingers, she unfolded the page – badly mended and finished off with wine splatters and tears. It didn't matter. She knew they would love it anyway. They would be able to see it for what it really was – all her love and grief poured onto the page with the paint.

Dropping to one knee in front of the little lavender

bush, Rowan scooped the earth away with her hands. Then, with gentle fingers, she folded the painting back up, kissed it and laid it in the hole before gently covering it with Crumcarey's soil.

~

The first thing she saw as she pulled into the carpark near the top of Craigie Head was Olive's hire-tractor. So *that's* how Peter had decided to make his way up to their rendezvous point, was it? She shook her head and grinned. Well… top marks!

Rowan hurried along the winding footpath that followed the edge of the cliff all the way to the sea stack. It was the best place for watching the puffins as they came in from a long day of fishing. Peter had fallen in love with the spot when they'd come up here to work, and they'd both agreed they'd come back when it was time to celebrate finishing the book.

As she neared the stack, Rowan squinted against the low light as it painted everything gold. Yes – there he was, sitting on a tartan blanket and staring dreamily out to sea. Rowan's heart leapt as Mr Harris's words came back to her.

Suddenly, she had her answer. She knew exactly what she was going to do.

'Hi!' she said lightly, not wanting to make him jump.

'Hey!' he said, getting to his feet and grinning at her. 'Good afternoon?'

She nodded. She hadn't told him what she was heading off to do - just in case she had to chicken out at the last minute.

'I got the final painting done for you,' she said.

'Did you bring it?' he said, his eyes wide and eager.

Rowan shook her head. 'It's in the car... I didn't want to risk losing it over the edge!'

'Good call,' said Peter. 'What did you decide on in the end?'

Should she tell him? No – they could talk about that later when she'd had time for it to settle a bit.

'I'll show you when we head back,' she said.

'Brilliant!' said Peter. 'Congratulations, by the way!'

'You too,' said Rowan, staring at the hand he'd just stuck out towards her. Did he expect her to shake it?! She hesitated, and Peter dropped his hand again, looking awkward.

'I brought a bit of a picnic,' he said, pointing at the rucksack on the blanket behind him. 'There's a bottle of bubbly and a couple of glasses in there if I can tempt you?'

'In a bit?' said Rowan, feeling a swoop of nerves in her stomach. 'I've... erm... I've made a decision,' she stuttered. 'On the job?'

'Oh,' said Peter. 'Right... right, great!'

Rowan had to stop herself from laughing as his face went from hopeful to worried to blank and impassive in the space of a second. He was trying so hard not to influence her either way, and she was grateful... but all of a sudden, she couldn't wait to find out what he really thought.

'I've just got two things to check first,' she said.

'Okay...' said Peter, 'are they something I can help with?'

'I hope so,' said Rowan.

'Right... well, try me,' said Peter, running his fingers through his hair, which glinted gold in the sunlight.

'First one is - does the company have a policy against dating your colleagues?' said Rowan, watching him carefully for his reaction.

Peter's eyebrows shot up and he started to smile before turning deadly serious again. 'No... no, I don't think they do.'

'Okay,' said Rowan. 'Good. Because that might have been a deal breaker.'

Peter let out a bark of surprised laugher, and Rowan grinned at him.

'So... what's the-'

He didn't get the chance to finish the sentence, because Rowan had just tangled her fists in the front of his jumper and pulled him in for a kiss.

'That was the second thing,' she said, several minutes later, as she tried to regain her balance. Perhaps mind-blowing first kisses shouldn't be snatched on clifftops after all. Maybe they should add that to the guidebook!

'And?' said Peter, now grinning from ear to ear as he wove his fingers between hers, steadying her.

'I can't wait for our next project together,' she said, returning his smile.

Peter let out a loud *whoop* of pure joy that sent several Fulmars over the edge of the cliff, chattering grumpily at the interruption.

'Can I open the bubbly now?' he asked, sinking down onto the blanket and pulling her down next to him.

'In a sec,' she said, grinning and winding her arms around his neck. Peter took the hint. Wrapping his arms around her waist, he kissed the end of her nose and then pulled back with a smile.

'Tease!' she laughed.

Peter shrugged and moved forwards as if he was about to kiss her properly – but then he paused again.

'Look,' he breathed in her ear.

'What?' she said in surprise.

'Behind you!'

Rowan turned, only to come face to face with a little puffin that had landed just feet from the edge of their blanket. It was watching her curiously and she smiled at it before turning back to Peter.

'Don't worry,' he said, 'I'm sure it's not going to tell anyone.'

'As far as I'm concerned,' she said, leaning in to drop a tiny kiss on his lips, 'it can tell the entire island.'

THE END

ALSO BY BETH RAIN

Standalones:

How to be Angry at Christmas

Little Bamton Series:

Little Bamton: The Complete Series Collection: Books 1 - 5

Individual titles:

Christmas Lights and Snowball Fights (Little Bamton Book 1)

Spring Flowers and April Showers (Little Bamton Book 2)

Summer Nights and Pillow Fights (Little Bamton Book 3)

Autumn Cuddles and Muddy Puddles (Little Bamton Book 4)

Christmas Flings and Wedding Rings (Little Bamton Book 5)

Upper Bamton Series:

Upper Bamton: The Complete Series Collection: Books 1 - 4

Upper Bamton Series:

A New Arrival in Upper Bamton (Upper Bamton Book 1)

Rainy Days in Upper Bamton (Upper Bamton Book 2)

Hidden Treasures in Upper Bamton (Upper Bamton Book 3)

Time Flies By in Upper Bamton (Upper Bamton Book 4)

Crumcarey Island Series:

Christmas on Crumcarey (Crumcarey Island Book 1)

All Change on Crumcarey (Crumcarey Island Book 2)

Making Waves on Crumcarey (Crumcarey Island Book 3)

Fool's Gold on Crumcarey (Crumcarey Island Book 4)

Seabury Series:

Welcome to Seabury (Seabury Book 1)

Trouble in Seabury (Seabury Book 2)

Christmas in Seabury (Seabury Book 3)

Sandwiches in Seabury (Seabury Book 4)

Secrets in Seabury (Seabury Book 5)

Surprises in Seabury (Seabury Book 6)

Dreams and Ice Creams in Seabury (Seabury Book 7)

Mistakes and Heartbreaks in Seabury (Seabury Book 8)

Laughter and Happy Ever After in Seabury (Seabury Book 9)

A Quiet Life in Seabury (Seabury Book 10)

In A Spin in Seabury (Seabury Book 11)

Living The Dream in Seabury (Seabury Book 12)

Seabury Series Collections:

Kate's Story: Books 1 - 3

Hattie's Story: Books 4 - 6

Standalones: Books 7 - 9

Writing as Bea Fox:

What's a Girl To Do? The Complete Series

Individual titles:

The Holiday: What's a Girl To Do? (Book 1)

The Wedding: What's a Girl To Do? (Book 2)

The Lookalike: What's a Girl To Do? (Book 3)

The Reunion: What's a Girl To Do? (Book 4)

At Christmas: What's a Girl To Do? (Book 5)

ABOUT THE AUTHOR

Beth Rain has always wanted to be a writer and has been penning adventures for characters ever since she learned to stare into the middle-distance and daydream.

She has recently moved to a windswept, Scottish island, and it is a dream come true to spend her days hanging out with Bob – her trusty laptop – scoffing crisps and chocolate while dreaming up swoony love stories for all her imaginary friends.

Beth's writing will always deliver on the happy-ever-afters, so if you need cosy... you're in safe hands!

Visit www.bethrain.com for all the bookish goodness and keep up with all Beth's news by joining her monthly newsletter!

facebook.com/BethRainBooks
twitter.com/bethrainauthor
instagram.com/bethrainauthor

Printed in Great Britain
by Amazon